THE DISSIDENT WORD

THE DISSIDENT WORD

The Oxford Amnesty Lectures 1995

Chris Miller, EDITOR

 **BasicBooks**
A Division of HarperCollins*Publishers*

Designed by Joan Greenfield

Library of Congress Cataloging-in-Publication Data
The dissident word / Chris Miller, editor.
      p.   cm. — (Oxford Amnesty lectures; 1995)
    Includes bibliographical references and index.
    Contents: Introduction / Chris Miller — The writer as witch /
André Brink — Unholy words and terminal censorship / Wole
Soyinka — Gay autofiction / Edmund White — The oppressor
and the oppressed / Taslima Nasreen — On chaos / Gore Vidal
— Dissidence and creativity / Nawal El Saadawi.
    ISBN 0-465-01725-8
    1. Literature and society.   2. Conformity.   I. Miller, Chris.
II. Series.
PN51.D52   1995
808.8'59358—dc20   95-42213
                                                                CIP

96 97 98 99 ❖/HC 9 8 7 6 5 4 3 2 1

CONTENTS

PREFACE TO THE OXFORD
AMNESTY LECTURES

A single idea governs the Oxford Amnesty Lectures. Speakers of international reputation are invited to lecture in Oxford on a subject related to human rights. The public is charged to hear them. In this way funds are raised for Amnesty International, and the profile of human rights is raised in the academic and wider communities.

The organization of the lectures is the work of a group of Amnesty supporters. They act with the approval of Amnesty International, but are independent of it. Neither the themes of the annual series nor the views expressed by the speakers should be confused with the views of Amnesty itself. For each annual series a general theme is proposed, bringing a particular discipline or perspective to bear on human rights. The speakers are invited to submit an unpublished lecture, which is delivered in Oxford; the lectures are then published as a book.

Amnesty International is a worldwide voluntary movement that works to prevent some of the gravest violations by governments of people's fundamental human rights. Its 1.1 million members campaign to: free all prisoners of conscience—people detained anywhere for their beliefs or because of their ethnic origin, sex, color, or language, who have not used or advocated violence; ensure fair and prompt trials for political prisoners; abolish the death penalty, torture, and other cruel treatment of prisoners; end extrajudicial executions and "disappearances." Amnesty International also opposes abuses by opposition groups: hostage-taking, torture, and killings of prisoners and other arbitrary killings. Amnesty International, recognizing that human rights are indivisible and interdependent, works to promote all the human rights enshrined in the

Universal Declaration of Human Rights and other international standards, through human rights education programs and campaigning for the ratification of human rights treaties. Amnesty International is impartial: it is independent of any government, political persuasion, or religious creed. It does not support or oppose any government or political system, nor does it support or oppose the views of the victims whose rights it seeks to protect. It is concerned solely with the protection of the human rights involved in each case, regardless of the ideology of the government, opposition forces, or the beliefs of the individual.

Members of the Committee of the Oxford Amnesty Lectures 1995 were Madeleine Forey, John Gardner, Ewen Green, Chris Miller, Fabienne Pagnier, and Stephen Shute.

ACKNOWLEDGMENTS

The editing of so various a volume made recourse to well-informed others a necessity. With one exception, none of the essays as presented were annotated, and the production of notes was thus a collaborative effort between contributors and editor for the most part. If these have erred on the generous side, it was in order to open up the field to the attentive reader; for this reason, a current rather than a first edition has been preferred in most cases. My thanks to the Houghton Library, Harvard University, for permission to quote from the manuscript of John Jay Chapman's essay on Plato. I should like to thank Robert Smith, Robert White, Professor J. Reed, Andrew MacKinnon, Dinah Manisty, Richard Gartner, Donna Bagdasarian of *Arion*, and Richard Canning for their help in tracing quotations and explicating references, Ubaid Ansari for help with electronic media, and Madeleine Forey, John Gardner, Mohammed Mahmoud, and Wes Williams for reading and criticizing the Introduction; many of their suggestions have been adopted. Remaining errors are my own. The contributors have been very patient in again and again answering "one last question," and I am most grateful to them.

INTRODUCTION

Chris Miller

Lasst uns niederfahren
in der Sprache der Engel
zu den zerbrochenen Ziegeln Babels[1]

I

We speak a "fallen" language; the word that was with God was God, and we are not. Our naming of the world is a perpetual creation. This is not merely a theory of language, it is also a history of science, and a regulator, as we shall see, of the political role of religion. For the religions that specify man's metaphysical condition take account of the physical; the religious worldview is timeless, *eppure si muove*.[2] Religions also hear of political renamings, though they resist them. Callimachus stated "From Zeus come kings";[3] Sir Robert Filmer (1588–1653) argued for the divine right of kings; but Zeus has vanished, the Catholic Church of today has no brief for monarchy, and the Anglican Church is uncertain whether a divorced king can be even its nominal head. The movement of history can transform the "language of God" into a confined and essentialist code.

The creative word is distinctive, and our creative voices are dissentient by this token; this much is a truism. But do we not confine the creative by presenting it as dissident, and belie history in some measure?[4] Much art has, after all, been made in a metaphysical perspective, in which human experience may always and everywhere be the same. Yet the universalizing morality that religions prescribe is necessarily casuistic in practice, as it involves the accommodation of competing interests; politics is the theory of that accommodation at the civic level. The variety of human experience is, in short, a political fact, which the creative word cannot help but reflect.

A totalitarian context focuses the political in and on the creative. For the West, the term *dissidence* is primarily associated with the intellectual resistance to what we might call the Soviet empire, and the paradigm afforded by such resistance was a very sympathetic one. The nature of Soviet totalitarianism allowed an unconditional sympathy for dissidents. Resistance to it seemed transparently a moral issue, and was theorized as such. Here was a system whose founding principles survived only in a wooden jargon, while the daily experience of its citizens made the state's sloganeering language, paradoxically, into a criterion of truth.

Sympathy for this dissidence was easy, though the term *Soviet empire* was sometimes contested. I believe the term was justified. Analogies will emerge, I think, in the presentation of a "dissident" at first sight less sympathetic, who is briefly mentioned in the contribution of Taslima Nasreen. He is Netaji Subhas Chandra Bose (*Netaji* is Hindi for "respected leader") and he was born on January 23, 1877. Among the most distinguished Indian nationalists, he is best known for an act that even now is likely to arouse mixed feelings in the Western reader. In October 1943, he proclaimed an Independent Indian Government and, with Japanese backing, advanced on India with three divisions each of ten thousand soldiers, and twenty thousand volunteers, all recruited among Indian prisoners of the Japanese army. Defeated near Kohima for lack of Japanese air cover, he was forced to retreat. He is thought to have died in Japan after an air crash. Bose had fled India for Berlin, and initially been welcomed by Hitler. He had then collaborated with the Japanese. What title does he have to our sympathy?

His title is that of anyone fighting to free his country from an occupation. Gandhi called him "patriot of patriots." He was educated in Calcutta and Cambridge and, on Gandhi's advice, went to work under C. R. Das in Bengal. He was imprisoned for the first time in 1921; in 1924 he became chief executive officer of the Corporation of Calcutta, but was deported to Burma shortly afterward. He was released only in 1927. As President of the Bengal Congress, at the 1928 Indian National Congress Session in Calcutta he proposed a resolution in favor of independence; a similar resolution was passed the following year when Gandhi supported it. By the time the civil disobedience campaign began, Bose had again been detained. He was released, rearrested, and allowed to go into exile in Europe after a year's detention. There he wrote *The Indian Struggle 1920–1934* and attempted to promote the Indian cause among European leaders. On his return, he was again imprisoned for a year. In 1938 he was president of the Indian National Congress, and in conflict with Gandhi over the need for an industrialization policy. He resigned and was again incarcerated in July 1940; he was released when he threatened to starve himself to death, then escaped from house arrest to reach Berlin.

What choices did he have? The legitimate demand that an occupying power leave his country had met with repression. When he pressed his demands effectively, he was imprisoned, deported, or exiled. His allies were unsavory, but in war one cannot always choose one's friends. Britain and the United States allied themselves in the same war with Stalin's Soviet Union, with whose politics they were fundamentally at odds. Stalin's record with human rights challenged even that of Hitler, but victory in Europe would have been impossible without the Soviet Union. Bose would perhaps have had to contend with a Japanese army of occupation if he had succeeded in liberating India, rather as the resistance fighters of the Eastern countries were obliged to hope that liberation by the Red Army was not simply a new form of occupation.

This story appears here because the term dissident may evoke a certain complacency in the West; the "end of history" has occurred, and with it no doubt the end of dissidence.[5] (A similar theory prevailed, of course, in the Soviet Union.) It is a nationalist ideology that lies behind the Western reader's hesitation in praising Bose, taking the form of a belief that Empire should have fought on the Allied side (which it mostly did). That nationalist ideology has not yet been abandoned, and it is not excessive to detect it in most European literature of the period of colonialism.

To point this out is to some extent to point out the limitations of the "inherent dissidence of the creative word." Few writers have exhibited the anarchic inventiveness of Laurence Sterne (1713–1768), yet there is no sign in his work of any objection to the ideology of superiority that allowed Europe to conquer and exploit. The "sentiment" that he evokes in "The Sword. Rennes," an episode of *A Sentimental Journey*, arises at the cost of an invisible exploitation. Indeed, Sterne can hope to arouse this sentiment only because the exploitation is invisible. The Marquis d'E****, he tells us, could not sustain his name with the little his ancestors had left, and "there was no resource but commerce."

In any other province than France, save Britany, this was smiting the root for ever of the little tree his pride and affection wished to see re-blossom—But in Britany, there being a provision for this, he availed himself of it; and taking an occasion when the states were assembled at Rennes, the Marquis, attended with his two boys, entered the court; and having pleaded the right of an ancient law of the duchy, which, though seldom claimed, he said, was no less in force; he took his sword from his side—Here, said he, take it; and be trusty guardians of it, till better times put me in condition to accept it.

The president accepted the Marquis's sword—he stayed a few minutes to see it deposited in the archives of his house, and departed.

The Marquis and his whole family embarked the next day for Martinico, and in about nineteen or twenty years of successful application to business, with some unlooked-for bequests from distant branches of his house—returned home to reclaim his nobility and to support it.[6]

Sterne, who attended the ceremony of reinstatement, exclaims "O how I envied him his feelings!" The envy might have been shared by those enslaved for the Marquis's enrichment; to deal with them, he had left his nobility at home. But their experience has vanished. The possibility of the restoration of the Marquis's status depended on exploitation, which is not even a peripheral issue for Sterne. And this is not simply a matter of his historical context. The principles that might have led Sterne to perceive an experience other than that of the Marquis in "the story of the Marquis" were already in circulation. *A Sentimental Journey* is a record of the grand tour during which, in 1765, Sterne met Denis Diderot (1713–1784). Diderot was already engaged in the *Encyclopédie* and was contributing the attacks on slavery and despotism to Abbé Raynal's *Histoire des deux Indes*, which appeared in 1770. We can define this context more clearly by noting that the ideas of the *philosophes* and Raynal's work in particular strongly influenced Toussaint L'Ouverture in his successful revolt against French rule in another island of the (misnamed) West Indies, then Saint Domingo, today's Dominican Republic.[7]

II

Taslima Nasreen's account of the influence of Enlightenment ideas in Bengal, particularly among the followers of Henry Derozio, sheds further light on what we might call the "Sterne paradox." For those suffering the imposition of a foreign administration, the writings of Rousseau, Bentham, and Paine might seem relevant indeed, as they had for Europeans—within Europe. For Europeans outside Europe, Enlightenment principles to which they theoretically subscribed were not applicable to other races. Rousseau had said: "Man is born free, but is *everywhere* in chains."[8]

Nasreen gives credit to the policies of education implemented in the Raj. Yet the paradoxes of this system of education were several and they bring into focus many of the issues raised in this volume. Not least among these was that the need for education was first perceived because of the depravity to which Empire's early and isolated representatives were inclined. As Viswanathan remarks, "It is impossible not to be struck by the peculiar irony of a history in which England's initial involvement in the education of the natives derived less from a conviction of native immorality, as the later discourse might lead one to believe, than from the depravity of their own administrative merchants."[9]

The purpose of this education was undoubtedly to reinforce the ideology of racial superiority that permitted conquest in the first place. The difficulty was that the sectarianism of Indian society (itself a product of earlier conquest) meant that, until 1813, the English authorities did not allow missionaries into India, and the Bible was proscribed. Christianity was the moral superiority of the West; "we" had it, "they" didn't. And without Christianity, European ideas were liable to misinterpretation, it seemed. Alexander Duff states in his *India and India Missions:* "As Christianity has never taught rulers to oppress, so it will never teach subjects to rebel,"[10] thus concisely defining one of the more important roles Christianity has played in the Christian West. And the Reverend William Keane testified to Parliament about "political thoughts which [Indians] get out of our European books, but which it is impossible to reconcile with our position in that country, political thoughts of liberty and power . . . which, when they arise without religious principles, produce an effect which, to my mind, is one of unmixed evil."[11] Christianity is here seen to underpin a racist political hierarchy. A more extreme form of this combination was, of course, the underpinning of apartheid in South Africa. As André Brink points out in an essay written before apartheid had run its course, apartheid was not "simply a political policy 'adopted' as a response to the racial situation in the country, but had to be accepted as an extension of an entire value system. . . . The Church itself had to provide the ultimate justification for the ideology."[12]

Parallel to the debate about religion was one about language. Nasreen refers to the debate between Orientalists and Anglicists. This was important because, as Horace Wilson observed in his evidence to Parliament, "A mere English scholar is not respected for his learning by the natives; they have no notion of English as learning, but they have a high respect for a man who knows Sanskrit or who knows Arabic."[13] We have only to put this observation alongside Thomas Macaulay's views of the native culture—"These are the systems under the influence of which the people of India have become what they are. . . . To perpetuate them, is to perpetuate the degradation and misery of the people. Our duty is not to teach, but to unteach them"[14]—to realize that the choice of English as the medium of instruction was also intended to increase respect for the "mere English scholar" or mere Englishman. In fairness it must be added that prospects of individual advancement and the efficacy of the Western episteme had produced a demand for English-language teaching.

A contextualization for this choice is provided by the reaction of the British authorities in Kenya to the rise of nationalist sentiment and Mau Mau insurgency. Until the declaration of the state of emergency, some schools, missionary and nationalist alike, had taught in the native languages; in 1952, all schools were taken over by the District Education Boards chaired by Englishmen. In the words of the Kenyan novelist and playwright Ngũgĩ wa Thiong'o, "English became the language of . . . formal education. In Kenya, English became more than a language; it was *the* language, and all others had to bow before it in deference."[15] Ngũgĩ goes on to explain that "one of the most humiliating experiences was to be caught speaking Gikuyu in the vicinity of the school. The culprit was given corporal punishment—three to five strokes of the cane on bare buttocks—or was made to carry a metal plate around the neck with inscriptions such as I AM STUPID or I AM A DONKEY."[16] In this manner too the superiority of the "mere English scholar" or mere English colonialist was reinforced.

What could be taught in India to cement the moral superiority of the English race, if direct indoctrination with Christianity was ruled out? Viswanathan observes that "under no circumstances was the Bentinck administration or any other administration following his willing to support Oriental learning if it meant the perpetuation of Oriental languages and literature as the source of intellectual values, moral and religious."[17] The answer, of course, was English literature, which contained, apparently, all the values required. And though *Tristram Shandy* may not have seemed a perfect vehicle for demonstrating the moral superiority of the English people, it is clear that neither it nor *A Sentimental Journey* were likely to produce instances of objection to colonial rule. As Ngũgĩ observes of his own situation: "Literary education was now determined by the dominant language while also reinforcing that dominance."[18] So thoroughly was that dominance effected that Ngũgĩ, widely regarded as one of the major literary figures of our time, still meets with great perplexity concerning his decision to stop writing in English and write in Gikuyu. "But Gikuyu is my mother tongue!"[19] Over the point of the exclamation mark hangs the pall of colonial history. Viswanathan concludes: "we can no longer afford to regard the uses to which literary works were put in the service of imperialism as extraneous to the way these texts are to be read."[20]

III

The purpose of these reflections on imperialism has not been to condemn either Western literature or Christianity. As Nasreen points out, the prospect of Indians demanding democratic institutions had been foreseen, and though it would mean the end of empire, was not wholly rejected. And Western Enlightenment ideas are very forcibly reasserted in this volume by Wole Soyinka, Taslima Nasreen, and Nawal El Saadawi. Christianity was once the language of the Inquisition; it is now rather more often the language of the "liberal inquisition."[21] My intention is rather to point out the complex connections between language, culture, and religion. Having offered, in Sterne, an example of the failure of a creative writer to criticize an ideology of his times (it will be observed that it was not his intention to do so, and this is the point that I am making), I wish to turn to another author not at first sight relevant, Samuel Richardson. His *Pamela* (1740–1741) offers a more favorable example of the inherent dissidence of the creative word.

Richardson was far from being a revolutionary, and *Pamela*, one of the earliest major novels of the English language, is not in essence a revolutionary work. In it, Mr. B, a grandee, seeks the sexual favors of one of his servants, Pamela. The novel consists very largely of Pamela's letters, recounting the episodes of Mr. B's increasingly violent measures of seduction. The interest of these lies in the fact that Pamela's refusals are inaudible to Mr. B, despite their constituting an inordinate number of pages. For Pamela is construed by Mr. B as devoid of any will that does not favor his own ends. In true Edenic form, he construes his own attraction as occurring by her fault, and thus by her will; she is thus "slut," "hussy," and most explicitly "sauce-box," and her refusals must be counted hypocrisy or bargaining for higher rewards. This bargaining is explicitly mercantile: her virginity is early established by her parents as a *jewel*[22] (a sub-stance more unyielding than sauce) of literally transcending value and the question is what Mr. B must pay for it. It emerges that only the sacrament of marriage will do.

The interest of *Pamela* in this context is the revelation that Mr. B is the first reader of Pamela's letters, which are ostensibly addressed to her parents. As in a twentieth century totalitarian state, whatever she writes reaches the authorities; all the means of communication have been suborned. She continues to write, for it is, ultimately, the authorities that she is addressing; she is a kind of legalistic dissident, in cautious dialogue with the repressive aristocratic state. Mr. B seeks, in Václav Havel's terms, to wrap "the base exercise of power in the noble apparel of the letter of the law,"[23] and consequently feels *exposed* by her letters. When he first dismisses her, it is because: "I can't let her stay, I'll assure you, not only for her freedom of speech, but her letter-writing of all the secrets of my family"[24]—essentially his misbehavior. When Pamela is subjected to private imprisonment, it is not only Mr. B's interests that are at stake, but those of his warder and accom-plice in rape, Mrs. Jewkes, and all others guilty of complicity with Mr. B's abuses of power. If Pamela is to join the ruling classes, their position will be an unhappy one.

Pamela's "happy ending" promotes the dissident to gov-ernment, and in doing so dissolves many of her objections to the hierarchy. But in objecting, in "Pamela's words," to the treatment Pamela receives, Richardson has raised questions of principle that the reader, at least, cannot dismiss. Pamela has pointed out that over generations one family may fall into obscurity and another rise to prominence; that all were equal once, and that all must face the same ultimate judgment.[25] These points constitute a rejection of the principle of aristoc-racy. She remarks of Mr. B's first attempts at seduction: "Well may I forget that I am your servant, when you forget what belongs to a master"; Mr. B has lessened the "distancy" between them.[26] This is essentially the point that sexual relations cannot honestly be conducted except in a relation of equals, and it is a revolutionary one. At the turning point of the novel, Mr. B quits the apparel of nobility, appearing in the literal nakedness of his phallic power, and it turns out that Pamela's refusal is, after all, sincere; the hypothesis of her hypocrisy is tested to breaking point. When Mr. B eventually marries Pamela, his justification is her outstanding merit; and when Mr. B's sister attempts to humiliate the newly married Pamela by reducing her to the state of a servant with the threat of physical violence, the readers' repugnance rests not so much on our knowledge of Pamela's new state as on a rejection of any system where these outrageous liberties may be taken with the dignity of anyone at all. Richardson does not state, like Paine, that: "Hereditary succession requires the same obedience to ignorance as to wisdom";[27] he does not need to. The moral authority to which Richardson restores Mr. B makes it clear that Richardson does not believe what Paine implies; but Richardson's imaginative sympathy has adduced these principles and made them indefeasible.

IV

To produce an analogy for twentieth century legalistic dissidence in the work of an eighteenth century author may be surplus to our requirements; the issue is simply the dissidence of the imagination. Pamela labors under the Edenic ascription of man's desire to woman's agency, an arrangement conveniently depicted by portraying a woman's head upon the phallic serpent. This inversion is paralleled by the Islamic custom of veiling the woman's body. Pamela accepts that she is Mr. B's inferior as a woman, and has internalized the requirement that her sexual and reproductive freedom is confined to a choice of marriage partner,[28] though it is the burden of many other Western novels that not even this choice was available. From a feminist perspective, which is, I hope, now widely accepted in the West, it is difficult to see in the religious ideology of the subjection of women anything more than the advantage of men erected on a metaphysical platform. The clear implication is that religion has hitherto sanctified a status quo that moral revolution has since rendered untenable, and it is to the credit of the Anglican church that it has learned some of the lessons of feminism. Lessons about the toleration of homosexuality are being learned more slowly, *eppure si muove.*

Pamela's burden is not irrelevant to the cases of Nawal El Saadawi and Taslima Nasreen. Nawal El Saadawi has been living in temporary exile in the United States, having lived in Egypt under armed guard because her life was threatened by Islamic fundamentalists. Paradoxically, she has in the past been identified with the fundamentalists under the blanket term of "opposition," and was imprisoned with fundamentalists under Sadat. "Sadat had ordered the mass arrest without trial of several thousand Egyptians, representing the entire spectrum of political opposition in Egypt, from extreme right-wing religious fundamentalists to members of the left-oriented, Nasserite Progressive Union Party."[29] Sharing a cell with fundamentalists, Saadawi was released on Sadat's death, an experience that she records in her *Memoirs from the Women's Prison.* Her "opposition" to Sadat took the form of a book, *Women and Sex* (1973), which she wrote when she was director of Public Health and assistant general secretary of the Medical Association. It was too frank an account of her subject to be acceptable to the government in the context of rising Islamic fundamentalism, and she was dismissed from her jobs. She had already begun her novelistic career with *Memoirs of a Woman Doctor,* serialized in 1957. Nawal El Saadawi's rise from a child of rural Egypt to doctor of medicine and high-ranking administrator was prima facie no more likely than that the servant Pamela should marry her master. It was also accomplished without loss of integrity; this was a dissident who could not be silenced by promotion, and she was first sacked for the expression of her views, then imprisoned. Her account of Firdaus, the woman who chooses prostitution for her freedom and kills her pimp, is in every way the opposite of *Pamela*; it is one of the unmasking of each taboo, each fear that woman faces in a voyage of discovery that ends, inevitably, with death. The *Woman at Point Zero* must be killed, for as Firdaus says: "They do not fear my knife. It is my truth that frightens them."[30]

Taslima Nasreen, also a doctor, began writing in 1975. Her poems, novels, and columns have never eschewed controversy, but the defining moment was the publication in 1993 of *Lajja* (Shame), a novelistic description of the anti-Hindu riots that occurred in Bangladesh after the destruction by Hindu fundamentalists of the four-hundred-year-old Babri Mosque in Ayodhya, India. The novel describes the feelings of the Hindu Datta family, who identify with the secular aspirations that Nasreen sees as integral to the creation of Bangladesh. The Dattas live a besieged life; Suranjon Datta's antisectarian beliefs are slowly eroded by his newfound solidarity with Hindus and his despair at the ineffectual protests of his friends in the secular parties. His sister Maya is kidnapped from the family home and vanishes without trace. The culminating point of the novel is Suranjon's rape of a Muslim prostitute, on whom he seeks to revenge the countless atrocities of which his community has been a victim. He immediately regrets his action and is "swamped" with shame.[31]

Lajja dramatizes the difficulty faced by a persecuted community that seeks to maintain a secular, antisectarian perspective. The offense caused by the novel seems to have derived from two points: firstly the calling to account of the Muslim community for religious persecution, and secondly the account of the rape of a Muslim woman. Neither point calls for excuse. The context of atrocities committed in the name of religion more than legitimates Nasreen's hostility to sectarian religion, while the rape scene is not sensationalist but a realistic representation of the fact that women are frequently made to suffer for and by the acts of men in a society in which they are treated as the lowest level of the human hierarchy. The scene is a single incident, narrated in its full horror; *Lajja*'s long lists of similar atrocities perpetrated against Hindu women are liable to become meaningless statistics, especially to hostile parts of her sectarian audience, without such description. *Lajja* is a fictionalized work of documentation, an *oeuvre de circonstance* written in great haste, and by which Nasreen's work, otherwise unavailable in English translation, has been unfairly judged.

In her *Nirbachito Column*, Nasreen takes to task the religious precepts that permit or prescribe the subjection of women. In one of these articles, she describes her meeting with a young woman savagely beaten by her husband for refusing him sex. The husband demands sex several times a day; the young wife is suffering severe vaginal pain, and therefore refuses. When she refuses, he beats her with electric cable. The husband shows Nasreen the hadith Tirmizi: "If your wife commits a grave error, do not allow her into your bed and beat her in moderation," advice he has conflated with another hadith: "If a man summons his wife to make love, she must obey immediately."[32] The culture of sexual subordination of women is justified and reinforced by religious precept. In another article, Nasreen quotes the Koran on a husband's rights, citing three suras of the Koran, each of which permits a man sexual rights over his or his wife's servants.[33] We are back in the territory of *Pamela*.

For if Pamela reports her attempted rape by Mr. B, she is unlikely to be heard; as *a* Justice, Mr. B is *the* justice that Pamela can expect.[34] And if the prostitute raped by Suranjon in Nasreen's *Lajja* reports a rape, she is still less likely to be believed. The conditions prescribed by Islamic law for a woman to prove that she has been raped are an insult to the intelligence of rapists. Yet there are important differences. Even if Pamela had proved guilty of fornication, she was not likely to be stoned to death. In Bangladesh, a woman risks being stoned if she so much as smokes in the street.[35] There is a difference of degree here, one which has affected Suranjon's creator. Nasreen, as we know, now lives in exile in Sweden with a substantial bounty offered for her death by a group of Islamic clerics. In this, she shares the fate of one of the absent heroes of this volume, Salman Rushdie. This is indeed, in Soyinka's term, the age of "terminal censorship."

Soyinka raises the issue of fundamentalism without referring it to a particular religion. He points to the Christian fundamentalists willing to murder abortionists in the United States, to the Zionist or Orthodox extremists who regard the massacre perpetrated by Baruch Goldmann as commendable, and to the *fatwa* issued against Salman Rushdie. He points also to the fanatics of animal rights who are willing to sacrifice human lives in order to advance the cause of animal welfare. Yet it is Islamic fundamentalism that presents the greatest religious danger to human rights in the world today, not least because Islam (in which fundamentalism is a disproportionately influential minority) is the fastest growing faith in the world.

We live, says Gore Vidal, in the Age of Chaos, and the Age of Chaos is the last age of the cycle that must, in Giovanni Batista Vico's metaphor, begin anew with a Theocratic Age. Christianity, I have suggested, has largely come to terms with the fact of secular government.[36] Islamic fundamentalism has, on the contrary, tended to lay emphasis on theocracy, on the imposition of Islamic law. It claims that its transcendental perspective necessarily outweighs democracy and other secular considerations, and it is a claim that has the merit of apparent logic and simplicity. How can secular statesmen have the audacity to oppose the will of God?

V

It is a claim that one might honor if the will of God were indubitably available to humankind. The claim is further made that the will of God is indeed available to humankind. But even if this claim could be entertained, it cannot be honored in practice unless God is willing directly to undertake the business of government. The god who acts through humankind acts through fallible agents, who must be open to criticism and correction. The arguments against theocracy are those that apply to all cases of what I would term epistemological totalitarianism, of which the West has a much respected tradition deriving first and foremost from Plato. We may define epistemological totalitarianism as dictatorship based on a claim to higher knowledge of how things are (and more specifically, how they ought to be): such knowledge allows the initiate to prescribe the institutions and practices that will be best for everyone, regardless of whether "everyone" believes or accepts this.[37]

The arguments against such institutions are well known, and have been most effectively marshalled by Sir Karl Popper. These arguments have to do with a variety of different considerations. Some of them derive from a tradition of argument in favor of religious toleration, such as the point that a person cannot, in most theologies, obtain salvation under compulsion; a person cannot be obliged to believe, and it is generally supposed that gods are able to distinguish between a statement made under duress and a genuine profession of belief. The state, therefore, even if it were the function of the state to ensure the salvation of its citizens, gains nothing by attempting to impose particular beliefs. Other arguments have to do with the function of the state, since no government can have exclusively religious functions, and whatever preparation it seeks to make in this world for the next, it must also make some provision for this world. What we require of the state will include justice, and justice in this world is best separated from the institutions of religion, which may be insufficiently concerned for this world and confident that any errors can be remedied in the next.

Great social projects based on instructions from God, must, even if we assume that they derive from an infallible source, pass through the hands of many before they attain execution, and are likely to become distorted in the process. If it is argued that God Himself will ensure their perfection, a question arises why any such project should be favored over the status quo, in which presumably God also had a hand, and which He could, if it were His habit, have brought to perfection no less; why indeed He chooses human agency, and this human agency in particular. A society decreed by God should, no doubt, be immutable; as Plato points out, the divine can change only for the worse. Yet the intervention of human agency means that no human project can even attain the perfection from which change would necessarily be deleterious. (It is a premise of our argument here that human happiness in this world would not necessarily be considered by the theocratic project, and this may in itself be thought to constitute a reason for objecting to it.) Thus criticism of the form taken by the theocratic project must be legitimate, and presents a problem in itself, one to which we must add the difficulty of change in the human world.

Revelation of the form of an ideal society may, for example, fail to mention inventions that the future had not vouchsafed at the time of the revelation (we may cite the example of "test-tube babies"). Attitudes to these must be established by those best informed about the theocratic project, but they, unlike God, are fallible. If their access to the godhead is presumed to be constant, a question arises why such access did not precede as well as follow the revelation of the divine project. It is clear that there is no provision here for error on the part of the interpreter of God, yet the possibility of error cannot be ruled out. Advice concerning the project must be accepted from those proficient in a particular technique rather than in theology, since God, when advising on the formation of a society, cannot be expected to specify the diameter of the pipes or the span of the bridges. Yet this advice, with its material aptness, must be balanced against theological considerations whose compatibility with it is difficult to judge. Material considerations must be made to satisfy divine criteria. Again, human fallibility enters the case.[38]

A problem of succession also arises, for the conviction of the existence of a divine project normally ensues from the existence of a charismatic divine, whose access to the divine behest is more credible than that of others who pretend to the same authority. We leave aside the point that his access to the godhead is thus apparently judged not by direct apprehension of his access, but by the values of the world in which he displays his qualifications. How is God's choice of successor (assuming that He continues to provide a vessel of communication) to be recognized? As a rule, the answer to this and most other questions is provided not by continuous contact with God, but rather by the provision of a text said to stem from direct inspiration, whose prescriptions are to be enacted by those best able to interpret the text. If all religious leaders were of equal authority in the formation of tradition, no divine law would be immutable; all changes would be of equal authority with the original project. We have arrived at an essential point here. Established religious authority is generally *textual*, and it restores us to the realm of language, creation, and interpretation from which we set out.

VI

These arguments are not set out in a spirit of parody. They are intended to show that theocracy is a misnomer. Direct government by an omnipotent god would require no intermediaries; theocracy is government by mortals. The politician who "opposes the will of God" has every right to inquire into the authority of its spokesperson, and if the will of God seems to run counter to the interests of the citizens in this world, the statesman may legitimately defer to the citizens' interests, for on that subject, there is a body that can authoritatively testify: the citizens themselves. It is not, perhaps, to be expected that religious hierarchies should be democratically appointed, even within their congregations; but in any contest within the temporal sphere between the will of God and the will of the people, the decision should favor the will that is able to produce empirical proof of its inclinations. Government is about well-being in this world, not the next, and as Soyinka points out, the omnipotent can be expected to defend his own interests, if that is his intention.

The objections to a theocracy are very similar to those that held against the "godless" Soviet totalitarianism, and the consequences of the institution of "theocracy" likely to be very similar. Like Plato's *Republic*, like theocracy, the Soviet system was possessed of a founding myth, which necessarily degenerated into a *gennaion pseudos*.[39] It possessed unique means of control through "state ownership and central direction of all the means of production,"[40] and was in this respect historically unique. In all other respects it was the standard epistemological dictatorship, in which, as Havel says, "the principle must embrace and permeate everything."[41] From this, two consequences arise. Firstly, the provision of expertise threatens the system, since the rulers must often choose between expertise and the principle or myth. If expertise prevails, the myth is shown to be fallible, and its authority collapses. Where the myth prevails, on the one hand, the wrong decisions are made, while on the other, ideological extremism tends to become a criterion for policy selection (in particular, the selection of cadres), creating a cycle of increasing extremism. Secondly, as Havel says "everyone who steps out of line denies it [the myth] in principle and threatens it in its entirety," resulting in oppression that ultimately seeks absolute conformity of conduct in every context. And he goes on to point out the "direct connection" between Soviet ideology and Byzantine theocracy: "the highest secular authority is identical with the highest spiritual authority. . . . The centre of power is identical with the centre of truth."[42] The parallel is again clear.

Where power and truth can be confused, it is generally power that "benefits." Here we may take our text from Soyinka's mention of the oppression in Ogoniland. The Ogoni people organized to demonstrate against the high levels of pollution caused by oil extraction in their lands. Oil accounts for some 95 percent of Nigeria's foreign exchange earnings, and the Ogoni have not benefited. Under these circumstances, the Nigerian government might have sought to redress the situation in favor of the Ogonis; this notion does not seem perverse in itself. In fact, another principle prevailed, that of silencing all opposition to the government. Pollution could continue unchecked—that was beside the point—but opposition had to be crushed. Similar priorities existed throughout the Soviet empire, where immense pollution damage occurred as a result. The *Black Book of Censorship in the Polish People's Republic* stated: "It is necessary to eliminate . . . all information concerning danger to human life and health posed by industry or by chemical substances used in agriculture. This prohibition includes actual cases of pollution of the atmosphere, water, earth, or food which are dangerous to life and health." Information about "mass poisonings and illnesses" could only be reported with prior approval.[43] A heritage of poisoned environments and low life expectancy has resulted.

Where power and truth can be confused, the attempt to reinforce power is often extended to the elimination of knowledge, whether in individuals or in the public domain. Such was the action of the Soviet Union in dealing with the intelligentsia of the countries that it "liberated" (the Nazis followed a similar policy with similar means). Left-wing Polish intellectuals fleeing the Nazi invasion sought refuge with the invading Red Army; almost without exception they were sent to the gulag. The massacre at Katyn was only one example of this intention to "decapitate" Polish society so that it would be docile under the Soviet-trained Polish leaders imposed by the Soviet Union. Deportation orders were issued for: "Persons who have travelled abroad. Persons who are in contact with representatives of foreign states. Persons who are Esperantists or philatelists."[44] This was the act of the "godless" communist society.

Today, in Algeria, the Islamic Salvation Front (FIS) is fighting a vicious war with the secular and supposedly socialist government, the Front de Libération Nationale (FLN). The FLN was the party of the Algerian liberation movement. Three years ago it cancelled elections in which the FIS was winning. Neal Ascherson has pointed out the horrible historic ironies of this situation. The FIS is murdering the intellectuals of Algeria: among the 6,388 persons killed by the FIS are 2,207 white-collar workers, 101 schoolteachers, 670 members of liberal professions, 689 civil servants, 21 journalists, and 350 businessmen. Its proceedings are exactly the same as those of the Organisation de l'Armée Secrète (OAS), the right-wing French terrorist group that continued to fight the creation of independent Algeria after France had effectively ceded sovereignty in 1962. The OAS leader, General Raoul Salan, stated the intention of the terror campaign as "to destroy the best Muslim elements in the liberal professions."[45] The FIS is now doing in the name of Islam what the OAS once did in the name of imperialism. The FLN will not cede power. And it seems unlikely that, if the FIS attains power, democracy, with its attendant prospect of being voted out of power, will be among its priorities. What is the will of the people to the will of God?[46]

It is scarcely necessary to insist on these parallels. In each of these cases, political institutions providing for political change without violence would not only have obviated violence but would also have benefited the citizens concerned. Theocracy, by definition, cannot provide those institutions; it will tend, on the contrary, to emulate secular dictatorships in confusing power with truth, and in using power to repress the truth where the truth seems at odds with its single, specialized claim to knowledge. The likelihood is that theocracies would degenerate into the crimes of wholly unprincipled dictatorships such as the Nigerian, where the ultimate motive of the ruling group (they cannot be called an elite) is simply the extraction of maximum profits in the predictably short time during which they can maintain power.

VII

What fuels the violence of fundamentalism? Some part of the violence perhaps derives from the imperialist practice discussed above of degrading or, to use a term familiar in human rights reports, "disappearing" the native culture. The Western scientific episteme continually proves itself in the production of medicines, technology, armament. The native culture is shaken by this episteme at the same time as it is declared inferior and repressed by the purveyors of the episteme. And the technological West shows little sign of registering as knowledge the practices of low-tech cultures such as nomads, whose methods of land-use nevertheless obey ecological imperatives that the West is only beginning to discover. Under these circumstances, what identity can the native culture assert? It cannot be economic; it cannot be technological; it must be traditional. In the case of Islam, it combines a warrior culture and its own history of imperial conquest with a transcendental perspective from which to condemn the morals and secular achievements of the West.

Impotence in regard to the West is, however, only one side of the question. The other side is the lack of human rights that prevails in much of the Islamic world for reasons quite irrelevant to the faith. The notion that democracy is "alien to the culture" of the Arab world might perhaps be put to a referendum in the relevant countries. The experience of voting an Islamic government into power, putting it to the test, and voting it out again if necessary, might also be revelatory. The imperialist West, for its part, continues, as Nawal El Saadawi notes, to demonstrate its military power in the suppression of insubordinate regimes (Nicaragua, Panama, Iraq), and its economic power in terms of trade and provision of capital.

To examine the new language of imperialism is therefore vital. As Nawal El Saadawi states, "protection," as in "protectorate," no longer carries much conviction in Egypt. And as Wole Soyinka points out, the term "pacification" has a history. Indeed, its imperial history for modern Nigeria is definitively summarized by its use in the last sentence of Chinua Achebe's *Things Fall Apart*,[47] in which Achebe's story of the destruction of native culture by white intervention is to form a footnote in the "history" projected by the English commissioner, a history to be entitled *The Pacification of the Primitive Tribes of the Lower Niger*. When Nawal El Saadawi mentioned the pernicious effects that are sometimes hidden under the word "development," many faces in her very cosmopolitan audience showed open delight, as they did when the term "structural adjustment" was arraigned under the same charges.

It should be noted that the most technical arms of the Western episteme have been made to serve an imperial ideology. Frantz Fanon, in *The Wretched of the Earth*, cites the case of Dr. Carothers, a World Health Organisation expert who in 1954 published *Normal and Pathological Psychology of the African*. In it, this "international expert" concluded that: "The African makes very little use of his frontal lobes. All the particularities of African psychiatry can be put down to frontal laziness." And Carothers makes himself clearer with a very vivid comparison: the normal African is a lobotomized European. This view, says Carothers, is concordant with the views of many other authors, each of whom arrived independently at the same conclusion. Fanon adds the useful information that Dr. Carothers defined the Mau Mau revolt as the expression of an unconscious frustration complex.[48]

Carothers may be thought to have betrayed the spirit of objectivity that should inhabit medical science. But in the matter of colonialism, the West has consistently betrayed its ideals. Its ideals are, after all, those of the Enlightenment, ideals of justice and universality. These ideals broke down over race. Edward Said, in his 1992 Oxford Amnesty lecture, cited Ernest Renan, a writer considered progressive in his time:

> The regeneration of the inferior or degenerate races by the superior races is part of the providential order of things for humanity. . . . *Regere imperio populos*, that is our vocation. Nature has made a race of workers, the Chinese race, who have wonderful manual dexterity and almost no sense of honour; govern them with justice, levying from them, in return for the blessing of such a government, an ample allowance for the conquering race, and they will be satisfied; a race of tillers of the soil, the Negro; treat him with kindness and humanity, and all will be as it should; a race of masters and soldiers, the European race.[49]

For Aimé Césaire, from whose *Discours sur le colonialisme* Said takes this quotation, Renan is quite simply a precursor of Nazism. The betrayal of the ideal of justice is explicit when it is associated with the notion of conquest as both blessing and exploitation.

Renan's "sense of honor" requires him to ascribe to Nature or providence (two carpetbags in which ideology is commonly accommodated) the creation of an unscrupulous Chinese race. Today, what we perceive in his ascription is a pretext for conquest, which history records as glorious, and which, as Conrad notes, "mostly means the taking it away from those who have a different complexion or slightly flatter noses than ourselves."[50] Renan is not, of course, alone. Hume ("the negro is naturally inferior to the whites"), Jefferson ("the blacks are inferior to the whites on endowments of both body and mind"),[51] Hegel ("Among the negroes moral sentiments are quite weak, or more strictly, non existent")[52] are happy to join the chorus. Hegel is very explicit: in reference to the African character, "we must quite give up the principle which naturally accompanies all *our* ideas—the category of Universality."[53] Shakespeare's Caliban, whose own language has been "disappeared" like Ngũgĩ's Gikuyu ("thou didst not, savage/Know thine own meaning, but wouldst gabble like/A thing most brutish"),[54] is often praised by contemporary African writers; he is at least allowed a voice.

VIII

But the attitudes expressed by Renan are less often publicly avouched today, and a danger to human rights, as Soyinka points out, comes from another kind of paltering. Its name is political correctness. If it can be defined, it seems to be the claim that any grouping of humanity is entitled to avoid stigmatization or exclusive definition under that group heading, though this claim tends to slide into another: that the group is entitled to positive representation under its group heading. Linguistic usage can reinforce prejudice, just as the demand for positive representation can constitute a demand for censorship.

Is political correctness, in part, a product of postmodernism? Jean-François Lyotard's "incredulity toward metanarratives"[55] has come to be the dominant metanarrative of postmodernism, and with it an account of culture in which human knowledge is described in terms of language games. Communication between these is inevitably limited; disagreement may be a failure to appreciate the rules of the game. (Lyotard's contention is, of course, occidental in scope. The evidence for incredulity in Islam, Judaism, or even Christianity outside Western Europe is limited.) Language games are a recipe for relativism, which political correctness clearly inhabits in the form of cultural separatism. As Ludwig Wittgenstein says:

> Where two principles really do meet which cannot be reconciled with one another, then each man declares the other a fool and a heretic. I said 'combat' the other man—but wouldn't I give him *reasons*? Certainly: but how far do they go? At the end of reasons comes *persuasion*. (Think what happens when missionaries convert natives.)[56]

Trigg, countering him, points out that this is to lay too great a stress on what people believe, and too little on "what is worthy of acceptance or rejection": "the main impetus to relativistic theories comes from the fact of human disagreement."[57] The discourses of conflicting cultures (*eppure si muove*) can come into contact, and representations can, in a civilized community, be argued.

Soyinka found that he had been "courageous" in advancing the case of Salman Rushdie, and in condemning the *fatwa*;

since Rushdie had offended Islam, his case was not defensible, especially by non-Islamic whites. Here, political correctness is working as censorship, and on this basis, freedom of speech will indeed be no more than a game. The same grounds will forbid Islam from mentioning that Zionism meant clearing Palestine of Palestinians, lest offense be given; it would be necessary to censor the Koran for fear of giving offense to feminists; it would be necessary to avoid mentioning this for fear of giving offense to Islam. White supremacists must not be confronted with any evidence of intellection within a colored skin. We shall not be able to refer to differences. Interlocution will carry too great a risk of disagreement and offense. We shall have to adapt Wittgenstein, and say, "What we cannot agree upon we must pass over in silence."[58] Tact will have become a truth-theory.

The very *reductio* we have given illustrates why the *fatwa* against Rushdie must be condemned. Humans do disagree. For reasons that we have already seen, it is not desirable that they should cease to disagree, and that all forms of knowledge and morality should thus remain exactly as they are— which is, needless to say, widely divergent. It is therefore not even *expedient* that people should be killed for the expression of their opinions. Taslima Nasreen is charged, under laws of blasphemy that were established by the Raj for the prevention of intercommunal dispute, with "committing" a critical description of intercommunal dispute. But the Raj meanwhile has faded away under the legitimate criticisms of those— Islamic, Hindu, Jain, and others—who found its theory and practice objectionable and said so. We might add that reference to the cases of either Rushdie or Nasreen does not involve exclusively religious or cultural issues. In the cases of both Rushdie and Nasreen, the considerations that led to the imposition of a *fatwa* were not, in any case, purely theologico-juridical, but involved political expediency, which is recognized in most cultures. Is Nasreen the only feminist in Bangladesh? Is Rushdie the only apostate author to have "blas-phemed"? (I hesitate to defy extremists to extend from their individual targets to a general hecatomb.) Those who now restrict the right of expression have inevitably sought it or benefited from it in the past.

Postmodernism and political correctness agree on an atomized account of culture, one associated with what Gore Vidal calls "the dramatic migration of the tribes": the move-ment of peoples across national frontiers, and the assertion of national and regional identity within the existing nation-states. It is this atomism that enables Nawal El Saadawi to equate postmodernism with tourism, perceiving in both a kind of consumerism. If language games are all incommuni-cable and interchangeable, peregrine postmodernists may seek out the most "authentic" or "hybrid" or simply the cutest "game." They become cultural tourists, moving effort-lessly between cultures which form the object of their decisive metalanguage. This form of tourism reduces cultures to a spectacle. The language games played by such cultural tourists are rather rarefied relative to the cultures about which they are played, as Nawal El Saadawi notes; the consumer is incomprehensible to the consumed, even in translation. On the whole, the connoisseur of this kind is well aware that the game is arcane. "Theory" does not always seek to explain itself with maximum clarity.

IX

I have made it clear that I do not believe religious beliefs to be entirely timeless, and that I hold this to be a respectable attribute. The examples we have noted, in which Christianity has served to sanction in imperialism a social order that it would now (for the most part) reprove, and has accommo-dated in some degree a feminism it would previously have rejected, are not solitary ones. And it is not my intention to suggest that Christianity has only ever served reactionary causes, though the essentialism of religions makes them necessarily conservative for the most part. Religion cannot allow too free an interpretation of its text, lest it cease to exhibit any unity; it must say, with Jacques Derrida, but for exactly opposite reasons, that there is no *hors texte*; and it must nevertheless accommodate the existence of one.

This might in itself be a paradigm of the skill of interpretation, and to interpretation and English literature we return. Nawal El Saadawi draws our attention to the strange, dialectical relations between Satan and God. For, as she says, the devil has no power relative to God, but is responsible for disaster, defeat, and misery, while God, who has all the power, is not responsible for any of these things. And she identifies Satan with the dissident other. We have already seen how this model is transposed, in the Christian symbolology of *Pamela* and the Islamic institution of the veil, to women. In the three monotheistic religions, men have all the power, but blame their desire upon women. In a dialectic which is essentially that of men's relation to their own desire, women are first decreed pure of all desire, then condemned as sluts for the desire they are said to excite whether or not they encourage it.

The convergence of these two models, of evil deriving from woman and of the devil as dissident, are the core of that very Christian work, Milton's *Paradise Lost*. The structures it exhibits are so material to what we have already said about theocracy and dissidence that the coincidence deserves to be explored. In Milton's account, Satan has objected to an essentialist hierarchy of power, rejected the *gennaion pseudos* of theocracy, and fomented a rebellion. Satan's motives may not be democratic (this is a *coup de palais* rather than a proletarian revolution); but the accusation of envy is an eternal cliché in the mouth of the power-holders. Satan's revolution is compromised by violence, but, to quote Soyinka's statement in his prison notes, *The Man Died,* "Those who make peaceful change impossible make violent change inevitable."[59] Milton's account of metaphysical right inevitably vindicated by force majeure does God no favors. But once the question of authority has been raised, there is no alternative; we are not expecting God to attempt to legitimize His rule by holding elections. That might mean power finishing up in the "wrong hands," always assuming that in this case power is transferable. If it is not, God's metaphysical title does seem reducible to force majeure. This is a god who decrees torture and makes it last. Don't mess with him.

The contest is between the omnipotent and some of his minions, and might lead us to expect a shorter book. But when we enter this narrative, the coup attempt has already been defeated, and is recounted only in flashback. The question now is only of forms of resistance or surrender. Here Milton is famously "a true Poet and of the Devil's party without knowing it."[60] For it becomes clear that dissidence, like the fallen angels, is immortal. The omnipotent himself cannot dispose of dissidence, let alone those less qualified for repression. Marginal, repressed, tortured—dissidence continues. Soyinka, echoing the fallen angels' debate, writes in the context of the current Nigerian dictatorship: "The current phase of despondency is understandable; one does not see the tentative foundations of one's nation smashed repeatedly by juggernauts out of control without an acute sense of futility. Yet the alternative, to abandon one's goals, is such a negation of existence that one can only view it as worse than physical annihilation."[61] This is close to the fallen angel Moloc's argument.

Such a reading not only bears out Blake's contention (the "true poet" as necessarily dissident), it also demonstrates the limitations (and contradictions) of this kind of dichotomy. Satan, it can be seen, is no more the source of evil than God. Who made Satan? As Blake also said, "this history has been adopted by both parties," and reflects only mutual misunderstanding. The institutions of God are unsatisfactory; guerrilla war is likely to continue. Milton's paradigm applies as strongly to the United States venturing into Vietnam as to aspiring theocrats.

X

The form of reading given to *Paradise Lost* here is a less sophisticated variant of that which André Brink uses in his analogy between the writer and the witch. Brink's scrupulous reading points in *Macbeth* to the power of the marginalized, which lies not least in the stigmatization of the margins by the center. The witches are regarded as perverting Macbeth, but the "perversion" perceived in them is also a function of their marginalization. As Brink has said elsewhere: "When the conspiracy of lies surrounding me demands of me to silence the one word of truth given to me, *that word becomes the one word I wish to utter above all others.*"[62] It is in this reduction to a single word or slogan that the danger of perversion from free and full expression lies.

That which the center forbids gains in power. Taslima Nasreen became a world figure at the moment in which she was forced into exile. Salman Rushdie became known to many whom his writings had not reached when the *fatwa* was announced; has any other writer equal notoriety in the Islamic world? Brink himself demonstrates this point clearly. His *Looking on Darkness*, written in Afrikaans, was banned in 1974 by the South African government. What was the effect?

> Not only do my books sell more copies in South Africa than before they were hit by the censors (and banned books, too, continue to circulate at a dizzy pace), but the threat of being censored in Afrikaans, which would effec-

tively deprive me of my habitual readers, prompted me, as a measure of literary survival, to start writing in English as well. The result is that books previously available only in Afrikaans are now published in some twenty different countries. (And because they are in English, they are now, for the first time, being read by Black readers in South Africa too, as well as being translated into indigenous languages.) In several countries, a new awareness of South African writing has grown precisely because of the publicity given to the workings of censorship.[63]

Brink's view of *Macbeth* is of an Ur-site of feminism. Yet his implicit account of the way in which the marginal slowly impresses its values upon the center, of the way in which the dialectic is finally transcended, might hold equally of South Africa. Shelley describes Milton's devil as "one who perseveres in some purpose which he has conceived to be excellent in spite of adversity and torture,"[64] and this might well apply to the resistance to apartheid in South Africa. Everything from economics to firepower, the apartheid God included, dictated the failure of the black resistance: everything except justice. Against justice, force majeure was not enough. But we must remember, at the moment of triumph, Blake's dictum of the "history adopted by both parties." Though in South Africa the dialectic seems to have been largely overcome, dissidence is immortal. The margins necessarily remain. Not even in the overwhelming reconciliation that has occurred in South Africa has history come to an end. In a recent interview, Brink warned that the African National Congress also has a tendency to censor.[65]

As Brink says, literature must be for and not just against. It is the burden of all the texts in this volume that the dialectic we have perceived in *Paradise Lost* is itself restrictive, is a device that allows "the other" to be condemned unheard, and that it must be transcended. The writer's grasp and vision of wholeness, of alterity, and inclusion, these too are vital, even where, as in *Paradise Lost*, they are unwittingly displayed. Tolerance at this point treads a delicate line. As Soyinka says, "understanding" must not mean that we do not resist unfreedoms or oppression. We have the right, indeed the obligation, to condemn the *fatwa* against Rushdie. But this must not be done out of the perception that those who instigated the *fatwa* are evil. It must be done in order to defend values that we feel our opponents may, in fact, share: values of democracy, for example, for which many gave their lives under the Shah's rule; values of freedom from conquest for which many gave their lives in the Iraq-Iran war; values of freedom of speech and action, which all human communities seek, and from which the groups now in power in Iran benefited when they were in opposition in Europe.

XI

It is here that literature can help to inspire sympathy with "the other," even where the distance to be bridged is considerable. Emerson presents us with just such a distance:

> If an angry bigot assumes this bountiful cause of Abolition, and comes to me with his last news from Barbadoes, why should I not say to him, "Go love thy infant; love thy wood-chopper; be good-natured and modest; have that grace; and never varnish your hard, uncharitable ambition with this incredible tenderness for black folk a thousand miles off."[66]

(The question of distance is indeed integral to the failure of Western standards in imperialism.)[67] Yet the first-person account of one of these "black folk," that of Aimé Césaire, for example, might make such tenderness much less incredible, might indeed make it inevitable. In the absence of such an account, fiction may perform the same role, perhaps to even greater effect. A reader wrote to André Brink: "It was only through reading this book that for the first time in my life I discovered that black people are also human beings." For Richard Rorty, arguing a pragmatist notion of human rights, such narratives are the only way in which radical clashes of value can be overcome.[68]

Edmund White's account of gay "autofiction" is precisely of a mixture between fiction and the first-person account. The mixture reflects the desire to bear witness to a form of sexuality that for thousands of years has been forced to disguise its emotions under the cloak of accepted sexual relations; to the desire, in Havel's term, to stop "living within a lie." It also bears witness to the exploratory, heuristic, heretic function of literature of which André Brink speaks. What is homosexual experience? Here is a sexuality apparently without an overt literary tradition; and heterosexuals need only refer to the countless works about heterosexual love and desire that have confirmed and enriched their experience to imagine that an oppressed sexuality might feel the lack of such confirmation. In the twentieth century, a gay tradition is again under overt construction.

The very fact of prohibition is, necessarily, confusing to the neophyte practitioner. André Gide's *Corydon* sets out to prove that homosexuality is natural, and therefore not transgressive. In Jonathan Dollimore's description, "For Gide, transgression is in the name of a desire rooted in the natural, the sincere, the authentic."[69] Gide's argument implies that homosexuality is essentially natural, and transgressive only because society fails to perceive it as natural. For others, the transgression is itself the key. "Wilde's transgressive aesthetic is the reverse: insincerity, inauthenticity and unnaturalness become the liberating attributes of decentred identity and desire, and inversion becomes central to Wilde's expression of this aesthetic."[70] It is paradoxical to find this return to the dialectic of evil combined with the notion of decentered identity.

Rorty, in the article I referred to earlier, suggests that traditional answers to the question about why one should tolerate or care about "a stranger, a person who is no kin to me, a person whose habits I find disgusting" are inadequate. The traditional answer is, he says: "Because kinship and custom are morally irrelevant, irrelevant to the obligations imposed by the recognition of membership in the same species." Rorty continues: "This has never been very convincing, since it begs the question at issue: whether mere species membership is, in fact, a sufficient surrogate for closer kinship." "A better sort of answer," he believes, is the story that begins: "Because this is what it is like to be in [his/]her situation. . . ." For Rorty, this should be a sort of "long, sad, sentimental story."[71] The heterosexual reader of gay autofiction is not necessarily confronted with any such sentimentality, but with shared experiences in which homosexuality plays a discrepant but integral part. The work may not be didactic, but the process is called education.

XII

We began by saying that to confine literary creation to a role of dissidence is to cramp it, and to belie history in some measure. The creative work may differ from its predecessors, but nevertheless conform to an ideology or a faith and its standard representations. Miklós Haraszti points out that in the Soviet empire, more art was produced than ever. Little enough of it was dissident, at least in the Soviet context; on the contrary, censorship had become a dialogue between artists and authorities: "Partnership replaces dictatorship.

Enfranchisement ameliorates estrangement. . . . Today, every artist is a minor politician of culture. . . . Progressive censorship is simply the self-restraint of company artists."[72] If this seems frightening, we should remember the tradition of Western religious art and be partly consoled.

But even within that tradition, a progressive enfranchisement occurred, and by the time William Hazlitt had remarked that the "language of poetry naturally falls in with the language of power,"[73] it was no longer true. Dissidence is seen at its most overt where a totalitarianism attempts, as it were, to become epistemological: where the regime attempts to preempt the possibility of dissent by formulating an all-comprehending jargon in which only a conformist reality can be expressed. Here the dissidence of creative writing is immediately apparent, and, perhaps alone in such a society, bears the clearest mark of truth. In Argentina, Chile, and Uruguay, Departments of Sociology were closed because the social sciences themselves were considered subversive. In this way, says Vargas Llosa, "the realm of the imagination became . . . the kingdom of objective reality," and "our best teachers about reality were the dreamers, the literary artists."[74]

Such a context is confining indeed. The more profound dissidence is that laid out in the theory of language of which Roman Jakobson has given a classic exposition in "What is Poetry?"

> Why must we emphasise that the sign is not to be confused with the object? Because beside immediate awareness of the identity of sign and object (A is A_1), immediate awareness of the absence of this identity (A is not A_1) is necessary; this antinomy is inevitable, as, without contradiction there is no play of concepts, there is no play of signs, the relation between concept and sign becomes automatic, the course of events comes to a halt, consciousness of reality dies.[75]

We may compare Shelley, who says of poets that:

> their language is vitally metaphorical; that is, it marks the
> before unapprehended relations of things and perpetuates
> their apprehension, until words, which represent them,
> become, through time, signs for portions or classes of
> thought, instead of pictures of integral thoughts; and then,
> if no new poets should arise to create afresh the associa-
> tions which have thus been disorganised, language will be
> dead to all the nobler purpose of human intercourse.[76]

Jakobson goes on to say that poetry is "the fundamental
organiser of ideology,"[77] a sentiment akin to Shelley's remark
that poets are the "unacknowledged legislators of the world."[78]
This is the profoundest dissidence. To adapt Hazlitt's observation, ours is a century in which the language of poetry has
fallen *out* with the language of power, and repression has
become the poet's acknowledgment. The moral is perhaps
that when your government begins to criticize authors, you
should begin to criticize your government.

The form of acknowledgment that governments are
inclined to bestow is sanguinary, and I should like to end
with one of those stories that Rorty believes will impart conviction. I hope it will. Dissidence may be immortal, but dissidents are not. The story takes place in Buenos Aires. On
May 4, 1976, Haroldo and Marta Conti went out to the cinema, leaving their children in the charge of a friend. Conti
was a prizewinning author; the previous year he had won the
Casa de la Américas Prize for *Máscaro, el cazador de las Américas*. When they came back, a plainclothesman with a machine
gun opened the door. Their baby-sitter lay blindfolded on the
floor, his face a mass of bruises. The couple were beaten to
the ground with rifle butts and put in separate rooms. Inter-
rogation began.

At about four in the morning, one of the assailants made the humane gesture of taking Marta to the room where Haroldo was so that she could say goodbye to him. She was disfigured by the blows and her teeth had been broken. The man had to lead her by the arm because she had been blindfolded. Seeing them crossing the room, one of the plain-clothes men joked "Are you taking Madame to the ball?" Haroldo kissed Marta. She realised that he was not wearing a blindfold and was overcome with horror because she knew that only those who are going to die are allowed to see the faces of their torturers.[79]

Conti's death was confirmed in October 1980 by General Jorge Videla, then leader of the military junta. Others in Conti's position—ordinary people, not just journalists, novelists, and poets—can be saved by international opinion, and above all by words of dissent written not just by journalists, novelists, and poets, but by you, the reader of this article.

THE WRITER AS WITCH

André Brink

The request by the organizers of the Oxford Amnesty Lectures to supply a title for my contribution to this year's series of reflections on literature and freedom came at a time when I was preoccupied with one of my obsessive interests, *Macbeth*; and the easiest way of dealing with the request in those circumstances seemed to me to suggest as my title "The Writer as Witch." The difficulty only begins now that the goods have to be delivered. Still, in writing my novels I have often found the title a good place to start: on several occasions I have had the exhilarating experience of witnessing a whole narrative text teased into being by the need to respond to the challenge of that as yet open signifier, the title. I am sometimes reminded of the Finnish writer Herman Tikkanen, who began his career as a graphic artist with a special flair for titles; he only became a novelist when his titles became so long that they could no longer be accommodated at the bottom of a drawing.

The process of effecting a convergence of text and title is not as whimsical as it may appear at first sight, and in itself it may offer an illustration of the peculiar link between writing and freedom. Few other processes demonstrate so dramatically the fine balance of choice and necessity, openness and restraint that goes into the act of writing, and the fact that literary license does not mean licentiousness. For this very reason the literary experience presents a model for our explorations of freedom in other contexts: the social, the political, the ideological, the economic, the historical, ultimately the moral. Wherever, and in whatever context, freedom is tested and defined, the weight of moral choice is involved. I cannot conceive of a literary function without a moral dimension; even, and often specifically, in the postmodern text—which to many readers appears to be a flaunting of irresponsibility and pure abandon—the action inevitably acquires this "weight of moral choice," as I shall try to demonstrate. It is the particular consequence of the intricate relationship between the private and the public, and between the freedom of the imagination and the requirements of reason and of established codes of communication, that moral responsibility is invoked within the literary act. And this is also evident in an activity in which, almost without noticing it, we have already become engaged: that of matching text and title, a process of ludic accumulation and interaction, which in its own right requires a measure of wizardry, of witchcraft if you wish.

It is part of both the discipline and the freedom of literature that it permits of no absolute beginning (just as it militates against closure in an ending); even if we take as our starting point, as I propose to do, the witches in *Macbeth*, we have to take several steps back to prepare an entry into the text. For, as we shall see, the witches do not simply function automatically in the text, whether read or seen in performance: if they disturb and interrogate, as they so spectacularly do, all the assumptions of the patriarchal society into which they erupt from the first scene of the play, they bring with them the full burden of received notions and givens about witches and witchcraft. They are not there simply to endorse the attitudes of their audience (and to Elizabethans, witches were of course part of the social fabric of the time), but to question and subvert those attitudes. This, I would submit, already prefigures an essential aspect of the functioning of the writer in society. Among so many other things, what Lucy Mair says about witchcraft in her standard text with that title might just as well have been said about writing, namely, that "it reflects the fear of the hidden enemy that is to be found in most societies."[1]

The etymology of the word *witch* takes us to at least two different sources: the Anglo-Saxon *wit* ("knowledge"), which survives in our "wit" as it does in our "wisdom"; and the German *weihen* ("to consecrate"), with its overtones of "a sacrificial victim in a religious ritual." With the removal of writers or artists as soothsayers, prophets, and magi from the center stage of our modern secular society, we may be skeptical about regarding them as the curators of wisdom or consecrators of a religious function. But this is precisely what happened when the priestesses of a Mother Goddess within a matriarchal dispensation became branded and persecuted as "witches" in patriarchy. Which means that some observations about the writer as witch may be even more relevant than it might have seemed a moment ago. And if the notion of witch is extended to include, as it so often did in practice, the heretic, it will be even more illuminating for our discussion to bear in mind that *haeresis*, the Greek word for "heresy," originally meant *choice*, which made of the heretic "one who chooses." In our present context this would imply a choice against the power structures of the establishment in a given society; against the dominant discourse of the day; against the grain; sometimes even "against nature," depending on our definition of nature. Once again this adds to our possible readings of the witches in *Macbeth* and of the functioning of the writer in society.

In the traditional view of the weird sisters they are the instruments of fate, the embodiment of evil, possibly the extension and concretization of what is darkest and most obnoxious in Macbeth himself, consorts of the devil. (In this connection Jules Michelet's caution is significant: "In old European society it [was] very probable that downtrodden peasants thought they had more to hope from a pact with [the Devil] than from obedience to a God who seemed to have abandoned them.")[2] Certainly, through the eyes of most of the classical Shakespeareans (A. C. Bradley, John Dover Wilson, C. Wilson Knight, Harley Granville-Barker, and others), the function of the weird sisters is predominantly negative, subversive, destructive: by acting as the instruments of a supernatural force against which Macbeth is powerless, or at the very least by prodding his vaulting ambition and setting free his preexisting potential for evil, they pervert his nobility and—aided and abetted by their unwitting accomplice, his wife—effect the transformation of brave Macbeth, Valor's minion and worthy gentleman, into a tyrant whose sole name blisters our tongues. Yet another noble mind in Shakespeare's awe-inspiring gallery is here o'erthrown and quite, quite undone, another poet-philosopher turned into a bloody butcher.

But there is, of course, another way of looking at the role of the witches. Critics like Stephen Greenblatt, Peter Stally-brass, and others have focused an entirely new kind of attention on them. Terry Eagleton, in an essay that has drawn more than its fair share of vehement criticism, enthuses about them as:

> poets, prophetesses and devotees of female cult, radical separatists who scorn male power and lay bare the hollow sound and fury at its heart. Their words and bodies mock rigorous boundaries and make sport of fixed positions, unhinging received meanings as they dance, dissolve and rematerialize. But official society can only ever imagine its radical "other" as chaos rather than creativity, and is thus bound to define the sisters as "evil."[3]

Speaking as they do from a position of marginality and repression, their very presence—the contrariness and subversiveness that characterize each of their appearances—suggests that something is rotten in the state of Scotland: in a normal or healthy society witches, like ghosts, cannot function and do not appear; when they do, they become markers of a lack and a perversion in society. After all, "Ideology is haunted by what it excludes, subverted by what it subordinates."[4] They do not, of course, "represent femininity" as such but femininity *gone wrong*; if they appear to be hideous, offensive, dangerous, it is because society has not allowed them to function naturally or normally. In this particular instance they are portrayed in terms of what they most obviously threaten: patriarchy—that is, everything that is regarded as acceptable by the males who keep it going and the power through which they assert themselves. In this respect, as Stallybrass points out, "Witchcraft in *Macbeth* . . . is not simply a reflection of a pre-given order of things; rather, it is a particular working upon, and legitimation of, the hegemony of patriarchy."[5]

To understand this, one has to heed the argument advanced by Janet and Stewart Farrar:

> Patriarchy's first assault on the (Earth) Goddess took the form of subordinating her. Her acceptable aspects were put under the charge of male masters, mothers becoming wives (as Hera) or sisters (as Artemis) or daughters (as Britomartis) or being masculinized altogether (as Danae). Her uncomfortable or (to the patriarchal mind) frightening or dangerous aspects become demonesses (as Lilith), dragons that had to be tamed (as Tiamat) or glorious sorceresses who had to be outmanoeuvred (as Circe).[6]

A recognition of the witches as a *necessary*, in fact inevitable, force of dissent—a *vox clamantis*—in the Scotland of their time (as much as in Elizabethan England or, for that matter, in our postmodern twentieth-century first or northern world) prompts us to look again at the values of the world that make it possible for Macbeth to rise, to o'erleap himself, and eventually to fall. There is no *inherent* difference, I would argue, between the valor that inspires him on the battlefield to unseam, with evident relish, an enemy "from the nave to th' chops," and the urge that prompts his murder of Duncan and the river of blood through which he wades in the second half of the play. Both sets of actions—those allegedly demonstrative of valor as much as those that characterize him as a butcher and a fiend—are predicated on violent action, self-gratification, and the denial of otherness, specifically of female otherness.

It is no coincidence, as Janet Adelman indicated, that Macbeth himself should describe his advance toward Duncan's bed as that of the rapist Tarquin approaching Lucrece, an image that we know haunted Shakespeare all his life.[7] Nor is it unexpected that after the murder Macduff should invite the courtiers into the dead king's bedroom to "destroy your sight/with a new Gorgon," that other highly ambivalent female figure of male mythology. All signs of femininity, including the gracious "effeminate" Duncan, have to be removed from the scene patriarchy has appropriated for itself.

And we owe it to the witches that we are invited to see this truth behind the glib surface of the play. For in the final analysis, with the single exception of Lady Macduff, the only "normal" female in the text,[8] they are the only ones among all the *dramatis personae* who dare to speak the truth. When all else fails, and everybody—including the virginal wimp Malcolm, who has no knowledge of woman and therefore is clearly predestined to recommence all the errors that have landed Scotland in its dire state—conspires around the Lie, they are the ones who dare to diagnose the true nature of the sickness in their world. Everybody else subsides into "equivocation," one of the key words of the text. In this respect, quite spectacularly, through an observation of the role of the weird sisters, the writer's function in society becomes dramatically conditioned and defined.

In another way, too, the witches replicate the writer's function: they are the primary agents of change in *Macbeth*, and whenever the action threatens to slow down or a particular thread of action is unraveled, they are responsible for propelling it anew. In this respect they embody, even in what seem to be their most dire interventions, society's forces of renewal and regeneration. They are the dynamo that drives the play.

They achieve this through a dual process. First, they trigger a dialectic between past and future, which forces the main characters, above all Macbeth himself, to define and redefine themselves in their relation to these two temporal dimensions, on the still point of the needle where future and past are gathered. From the very first moment of the play they propel the action forward by not dwelling on what is but on what is yet to be: "When shall we three meet again . . . ?"

When they do meet again, after the battle's been lost and won, it is not to commend Macbeth, as Duncan has, for what he has done, but to direct his gaze toward the future, when he will be king hereafter, to face the prospect of Banquo's issue on the throne. In the next few scenes this function will temporarily be taken over by Lady Macbeth—whose unsexing of herself and whose bloody thoughts immediately link her to the sisters—and by the pointing dagger. But after Banquo's murder has been botched, the sisters themselves resume their prospective function—and the last part of the play consists entirely of the fulfillment of their prophecies (reaching even beyond the limits of the play to Shakespeare's contemporary Jacobean audience).[9]

But this tremendous surge of the play toward the future is possible only because, at least implicitly, in the terms we have discussed before, the witches are rooted in the past, in a time when the sterile dichotomies and binarities imposed by patriarchy had not yet come into existence. The persistent imagery of childhood may well be seen to fit into this picture too: the child who was being constantly confronted with the man he has become. From the instant when Lady Macbeth plucks her nipple from the boneless gums of a nonexistent child to dash its brains out, the child—including the issue of a king who wears upon his baby brow the round and top of sovereignty—cannot be said to embody a vision of the future so much as a reminder of a past innocence. (Or, if it *does* represent the future, then only that very remote dimension of it where past and future meet in a "round.")

Another dialectic triggered by the witches is that between introspection and outward action. In their own appearances the integration of speech, song, and dance is indicative of this holistic functioning; in the framework of the plot, their intervention propels Macbeth not only forward in time, but inward in space. He can no longer merely and thoughtlessly act, as he has done on the battlefield, but finds himself compelled to face his several inner selves; simultaneously he interiorizes external time, from the early wish for events to trammel up the consequence to the last great *Blick ins Chaos*,[10] "Tomorrow, and tomorrow, and tomorrow." What is particularly significant is that in the intense solitude and vulnerability of the soliloquies—and *only* in those moments—he reveals what, in terms of the value systems at work in the play, can only be termed his submerged "female" side, those aspects in which he is most hauntingly linked to the witches: not so much to the terrible hags—the guise in which they present themselves—as to the wholesome, sensitive, emotional, and more than merely rational beings they must have been before being relegated to the margin of the kingdom. (And the margin, when viewed through Derridean eyes, is of course itself the simultaneous experience of an inside and an outside.)

Both the dynamics of the action achieved in this manner, and the wholeness of its presentation, may be seen as further illustrations of possibilities to be read into the writer's functioning in a world that often threatens to engulf us either in mere sound and fury or in the mud of stagnation. And where our experience of the world tends more often than not to the fragmentary—visible with peculiar poignancy in scientific and academic research with its increasing emphasis on ever smaller areas of specialization—writers' grasp and vision of wholeness, as much as their imagining and inclusion of otherness, offer a kind of secular redemption from the trivial, the meaningless, the bewildering, and the broken.

It may be argued, of course, that the functioning of the witches in *Macbeth* leads to devastation and ruin, not to wholeness and regeneration, even more so if Malcolm's accession to the throne is not seen as a return to order and normality but, as I would suggest, as confirmation of persistence in the very errors of patriarchy that have caused the misery in the first place. And it is true that Macbeth's first step into blood is the direct outcome of the witches' prompting. Which, in a superficial or traditional reading, would indeed brand them as purely violent and subversive creatures. But surely the point is that nowhere in their first encounter with Macbeth do they prompt him to murder Duncan: it is he himself, conditioned as he has become by violent male action, who immediately equates the attainment of kingship with murder, and accession to the throne with the forcible removal of Duncan. And perhaps this is part of the larger process of signification at work in the play: this is what happens to society when the witch-writer's wit and wisdom are not heeded, or when they are interpreted selfishly or narrowly.

At the same time this suggests another aspect of the writer's function: not to impose a particular reading on the reader. After all, literature cannot pretend to serve the cause of freedom if it does not respect the freedom of the reader. Morality, like charity, begins at home.

In this lies much of the precariousness of writing. The convergence of interests in the text, the crucial encounter between reader and writer, is primarily, and above all, a situation of choice. It is the heretic at work, even at the risk of seeing this freedom boomerang on the writer. This is part of the considerable price that comes with writing: the risk of being ridiculed, ignored, misunderstood; the risk, certainly in closed societies, of being victimized and persecuted. The sting of the writer, as of the bee, is inflicted at the price of the writer's own life. (The sting of a bee, said Jean Paulhan many years ago, may not amount to much, but if it were not for that, there would be no bees left any more.)

It remains, at best, a thankless task. With Macbeth and his queen slaughtered and Banquo murdered, what witness remains of the intervention of the witches? What was there in it for them?

At first sight, nothing. That is, within the strict limits of the action of the play itself. But *Macbeth* is not a tale that tells itself: it is not the legendary tree falling in a forest, heard by no one. It is a play, written on the pages of a book, acted upon a stage by poor strutting and fretting actors: after the performance they go home with the memory of what they have done, who they have been; just as we, the spectators, go home remembering. If anything is to be gained from the presentation of the witches and their interaction with Macbeth, we are the ones in whom this must be consummated. We have the freedom of choice in what to do about it; but if we assume the responsibility that goes with freedom, we shall start looking for answers to the questions posed by the play. The witches challenge Macbeth; the play challenges us: our equanimity, our assumptions, our prejudices, our being in the world. And it is naught for our comfort.[11] *This* is why there are plays, and writers, and bees, in the world.

Several aspects that have surfaced so far deserve a closer scrutiny; and in the second half of my paper I should like to examine the questions raised against the background of the situation of writing in South Africa, inasmuch as it may be used as a pointer toward more general perceptions.

There is little need to dwell on the role of the dissenting word in the stifling context of apartheid. But there are at least two aspects of the functioning of literature in that closed society that deserve further examination: first, an evaluation of what literature has effected within the struggle for liberation;

second, the dangers, to literature itself, revealed by its role of oppositionality in South Africa.

It is as easy for those writers involved in one way or another in the freedom struggle to claim—now that the battle's been lost and won—that their role in dismantling apartheid has been vital and indispensable, as it is for those who wished to keep their hands clean to assert that apartheid would have been eradicated whether a dissident word had been involved or not. In other words, that the role of literature has been grossly overrated and that its real effect has been negligible (most especially if one considers that within the masses of those oppressed by apartheid more than 60 percent were illiterate; which means that literature could at best have addressed itself only to a small elite who needed no prompting anyway).

The problem is that these matters can simply not be quantified. There is no test, no instrument, to measure what has been achieved by literature. One has to rely on extremely subjective evidence—letters, personal encounters, hearsay—as well as on deduction and conjecture. Yet I believe the conclusions to be drawn from cautious reasoning, supported where possible by testimony, need not be wholly negligible.

On the wall of a bullet-scarred building in a war zone in Soweto, in what may well have been the darkest days of apartheid, the mid-eighties, a photographer friend recorded the large irregularly spray-painted slogan: CRY, THE BELOVED COUNTRY. The writer—presumably black, given the location of the graffito—may never have read Alan Paton, but his word had become an example, and a starting point, of resistance and dissidence. Ten years earlier, when the poet Breyten Breytenbach was imprisoned, he smuggled out a letter from jail to tell me that in the detention cells below the Pretoria Supreme Court he had found, scratched into a grimy wall, the title of my novel *Looking on Darkness*.

Again, the dissident word somehow seems to have found its way into a larger activist context.

More emphatic was the testimony, repeated many, many times, of theater audiences in the seventies and eighties who reacted to performances (often clandestine, fly-by-night performances) of plays by Athol Fugard, Percy Mtwa, Zakes Mda, and others by rising to their feet and shouting a reverberating *Yesss!!* whenever apartheid or its structures and officials were ridiculed, challenged, or attacked by the characters onstage.

The people who reacted like this had no need to read or write, nor did the thousands who attended poetry readings in all the black townships of the country, in order to be moved and inspired in a surge of solidarity that transcended the many differences of culture that otherwise separated them and were so diabolically exploited by the government to divide and rule. Unlike Western countries, where poetry has become an entertainment of the elite, countries like South Africa turned it into a medium of mass communication through which the individual miseries and fears and sufferings of the deprived could be galvanized into the articulation of communal sorrow and rage, which was then transformed into a resolution to prevail, and translated into massive practical programs of resistance. There were few prisons in the country—and this included death row in Pretoria Central Prison—where merely negative suffering was not alchemized, through song, into the positive courage to endure and ultimately to triumph; in most of these institutions certain individuals erupted into poetry, which would be recited at night through the bars of a single cell, to be repeated and multiplied throughout the prison. Much of it may have been, judged by traditional Western norms, crude, one-dimensional, seldom transcending the level of sloganeering, but in those extreme conditions poetry fulfilled one of its earliest functions by translating the mute cry of the individual into shared experience. This moved from posing the basic questions—"*Senzeni na?* What have we done?"[12]—to searching for meaning, to proposing strategies for salvation (whether in the form of religious faith and the belief that justice will prevail, or in the more tangible and urgent shape of "Guava juice," that is, the Molotov cocktail).

We still cannot quantify it. And certainly one should be cautious not to overstate its importance, especially when weighed against so many other factors ranging from international sanctions, to defections within the white army, to massive programs of civic and industrial action, to armed struggle. But it would be foolish to underestimate its importance. Victory was achieved not simply through the facts of the actions undertaken, but through the spirit, the mindset, the commitment that inspired those actions and made it possible for people to sustain them against great odds; and the verbalization of the cause, its motivations and aims, its moral bedrock, was indispensable for success.

A few lines follow from letters addressed to me through the apartheid years and which I have quoted or paraphrased before, not because they are in any way exceptional (most writers against apartheid could cite innumerable similar or better examples) but precisely because they are representative, to the point of being "typical":

- From a young white Afrikaner student at Stellenbosch University: "It was only through reading this book that for the first time in my life I discovered that black people are also human beings."
- From a young black activist in Mdantsane township: "There was a time when I just wanted to kill whites, because I thought they were all our enemies. Now I have read this book and I see that there are whites who feel like us and who understand us. This helps me in my struggle because we are stronger when we are together."

- From a middle-aged "colored" teacher in exile in London: "If I had read this book when I was younger I would not have left the country because it would have given me faith to stay."

I have said we should not overestimate the importance of this functioning of the dissident word. But I have also said, and this has sustained me through times when it was difficult to believe in a new dawn following the night, that we would be foolish—in fact, I think we would be denying our humanity—to underestimate what the word can do in the world. Indeed, apartheid may have been dismantled without the help of literature; the question remains whether it would not have taken much, much longer, and whether the cost would not have been much, much higher. I cannot offer you final answers; there are situations where even a nonbeliever is forced to fall back on some form of faith. And in one way or another each literary text is not just a leap of the imagination but an act of faith, in the widest sense of the word.

The second aspect of the witchlike functioning of the writer in apartheid South Africa I have referred to may at first sight appear paradoxical; but I feel strongly enough about it to have spoken and written about it many times in the course of the last few years of transition toward a situation of greater normality. This concerns the very nature of the oppositional literature South Africa has produced in the last half-century.

Everything I have said so far should have made it clear that I am in complete agreement with the view that literature has by its very nature a dissenting function in society, through its subversion of whatever dominant discourse holds sway at any given moment—even, and perhaps especially, when it has itself contributed toward the evolution of that discourse. That is why there can never be any final "positions" in literature: whatever position is occupied at a certain time, or in a certain text, demands by its very existence the deconstructive scrutiny of its contemporaries and successors.

And yet the dissidence, the subversion, the oppositionality of literature (of art in general) is never a simplistic or unidirectional occupation; mere, and simple, opposition is, in the long run, as counterproductive as complacency or endorsement. The witches do not confront Macbeth with the simple aim of destroying him, or even the Scottish monarchy. Unleashing the forces of patriarchy against itself is only a starting point; approached in a certain light it may even be seen as no more than a pretext (certainly in the literal meaning of the word, pre-text): patriarchy has to be destroyed in order to make possible a restoration of the fertile processes of life and of the world, which can function only when a harmony between female and male forces has been achieved. (And one should add, of course, that such a balance is never "finally" achieved, because it is not stasis but a dynamic equilibrium of opposed impulses that requires constant creative adjustment and reassessment.)

In the years of the South African struggle of liberation, literature may have played, as I have tried to argue, an invaluable role; at the same time there has been an erosion of the imagination. A dangerous movement from what Dorothy Sayers once called a "poetry of search" toward a "poetry of statement" took place as the polyphonic, polyvocal richness of literature tended more and more toward the univocal, suggesting an impoverishment of the language itself.

If it is true that literature is by its very nature dissident and oppositional, it is equally true that it can also dissipate itself in mere dissidence or oppositionality; and if an entire literature threatens to define itself purely in terms of what it is against, there is a real danger of forfeiting the very richness and polyphony that assured its cultural validity to start with. A worthy literature is not only *against* unfreedom but *for* freedom; not only *against* the lie in its many forms but *for* truth; not only *against* injustice, but *for* justice.

And it goes further than this: if literature is to fulfill its full potential as witchcraft it does not simply and superficially direct itself against the illness of society in small specific terms but in an orchestration of the ultimate concerns of life and death. The struggle against apartheid, in South African literature, was not merely an opposition against a specific system of institutions, laws, and practices, but against the whole concept of the misuse of power. A successful poem by, say, Mongane Wally Serote or Sandile Dikeni was indeed an outcry against precisely defined evils of apartheid, but ultimately its life depended on its quality as an outcry against the very existence of injustice and oppression in human society.

If, in its moral dimension, literature is a dense and textured form of resistance to power (much as the weird sisters in *Macbeth* find themselves in opposition to the power demonstrated by patriarchy), it means that in an intriguing way literature acts in opposition to impulses within *itself*: because the functioning of literature is itself predicated on a notion of power, the power of the word, the power of the pen, the power of the mind, the power of culture. This explains another dimension of literature, not as a destructive, but as a de-con-structive force.

As the situation in South Africa slowly moves toward a semblance of normality, the dissenting function of literature becomes—as is the case in all other societies that present a semblance of normality—less dramatic and less obvious. The clearly visible face of a monolithic enemy as the target of dissent has disappeared; the enemy is much less obvious, more fluid and amorphous, more difficult to define. This may lessen the tension in the literary field. Engaging in writing is no longer quite such a hazardous business as before; the threat to life and limb has been largely dissipated. A comparable situation within the kind of patriarchy confronted by the witches in *Macbeth* would be that of a benign ruler, someone like Duncan perhaps, coming to power, extending the vote to women, putting an end to the persecution of witches, even introducing a measure of democracy, while still ensuring that women "know their place" in the domestic context; allowing the queen some say in matters of state, but ensuring that there are enough boneless gums tugging at her nipples to keep her from becoming too demanding.

Just as the *essential* struggle for the emancipation of women in the new South Africa has to continue, there remain important functions for literature to fulfill—in that country as everywhere else. Because nowhere on earth is there a human society where some kind of injustice is not perpetrated, where freedom is not curtailed in one way or another, where the expediency of the lie does not at least from time to time suppress the demand for truth. As long as society is imperfect there remains a necessary place for the dissident word.

It is a matter of changing strategies, or resorting to other devices, not of changing the essential nature of the confrontation. The Russian writer Victor Erofeyev expressed it in a particularly apt metaphor when he said that in a situation of war one may find completely new and inventive uses for furniture: building barricades, hitting the enemy over the head, or stoking a fire to keep warm. But in peacetime furniture reverts to being furniture. And this applies to the word in the literary text as well: in the new South Africa, as in most recently liberated societies, literature need no longer function as Molotov cocktail, as a weapon in the struggle, but should now rediscover its literariness and redefine its possibilities— *with* the advantage of all that has been gained in the struggle. On a much wider front than before the imagination can undertake its leaps and explorations, still the implacable enemy of complacency, of the misuse of power, of resignation, of corruption; but also as the protagonist and the celebrant of the eternal moral and aesthetic struggle *for* the just, the true, the free, and the beautiful. This struggle may become more, not less, intense when it is directed not against a clearly defined external enemy but against the enemy within, against the enemy in the guise of friend and ally, who attempts not to do battle with writers but to co-opt them. The more obscure and masked power becomes, the more insidious the threat it poses.

The writer and the witch, in refusing to be commanded, will continue to conjure up new images and possibilities of life, each more potent than the rest. In the end, as in the beginning, their watchword is "Speak—Demand—We will answer,"—even if that answer may not be what we expected or what we should like to hear.

UNHOLY WORDS AND TERMINAL CENSORSHIP

Wole Soyinka

I do not think too many literate people on this globe were particularly baffled when the expression "ethnic cleansing" was forged in Yugoslavia. The events were shocking enough and, as usual, the images were too evocative of Nazi concentration camps to leave any doubt in the minds of most about what that expression was meant to conceal. After all, the cult of the political oxymoron—we may as well exploit that latest lexical fad of public discourse, but for a worthwhile cause—does, especially in its deadly actualities, have a very long history.

Pacification, for instance: so thoroughly erased from our minds is the lethal contradiction of this expression, that we accept it for its very deceit. The process of pacification is, of course, anything but pacific. Well, I suppose when two pugilists meet in the ring and one bludgeons the other into a state of coma, it is indeed a form of pacification. But at least both entered the ring as equals, contested on agreed rules, and one was counted out according to due process. The pacification of a populace is in fact one that pits Goliath against David—Yeltsin versus Chechnya style—with the rules of engagement of a one-sided gospel pounded through the skull of David, and the verdict pronounced by Goliath both during and after the contest. Most of the time, David has merely asked to be left in peace, or has had the temerity to insist on his own logo on his boxing shorts, or at least a reasonable share of the purse. We hardly expect to find David seeking absolute possession of the ring, though he most certainly will demand that Goliath take his stool out of his corner and return to his own; he will also realistically concede physical occupation of the two neutral corners. That concession is, of course, never enough, and may indeed be cited as a piece of impertinence that needs to be punished.

If, therefore, the Nigerian government is heard to claim, for instance, as it has done repeatedly, that its presence in the oil-producing area of Nigeria among the Ogoni people is to ensure peace in that conflict-racked land, the linguistic analogue is already in active mental storage.[1] Never mind that its results are manifested in the sealing off of Ogoniland for nearly two years, and the subjection of tens of thousands to a reign of unabashed, even boastful, military terror, the world must, as that government expects it to, recognize the act as a time-honored exercise of pacification. Almighty Goliath unfurls his banner of pacification and employs it to muffle dissenting voices such as that of the poet and journalist, Odia Ofeimun, who insists that: "the short and tall of the story is that the Ogoni matter is about a struggle for how Nigeria's oil wealth must be perceived and shared. The rest is shadow."[2]

We have to ensure that credit is given where credit is due; and again we must acknowledge the reign of that expression in a world where "credit" is claimed, indeed competed for, by all groupings in the trade of discreditable conduct, such as bursting into a crowded pub in Ireland on Halloween night to reenact the St. Valentine's Day massacre[3]—only, this time, on innocents. Or sending a busload of ordinary working men and women, peasants and their children to a fiery end: ordering them out of their conveyance on a lonely road, separating them by clan, color, religion, and even sects within one religion, and machine-gunning and macheteing to death those designated as "the other." Ours has become, beyond all question, the age of terminal censorship, and one of its impressive characteristics is the ability to manipulate public consciousness into an optimistic reading of the most blatant texts of criminality, through verbal opiates. Charity, they say, begins at home; so there I make my beginning.

One of the most memorable innovations in this new communication direction took place during the civilian democratic government of Shehu Shagari in Nigeria about twelve years ago. A conflict had blown up between the somewhat left-leaning government of Kano state, headed by Abubakar

Rimi, and the feudal authority of the emir. The program of that government, like that of Balarabe Musa in Kaduna state, was openly directed toward the liberation of the Northern populace from a long tradition of subservience to feudal authority.

Not unexpectedly, seizing on the first opportunity to demonstrate their tenacity, the feudal forces mobilized themselves. An organized mob marched through the streets of Kano, sacking the Assembly, government offices, and so on, hacking perceived enemies of the feudal status quo to pieces—all this methodically, in broad daylight, over a period of hours, and without any interruption by the police. Among the victims of this rampage was a young radical social scientist and polemicist, Bala Mohammed, who was also one of the governor's close advisers. The feudal censors had decreed that he must be permanently silenced.

What was most chilling about the manner of his death was not so much the brutality of it but the deliberate, almost slowed-down tempo of the execution. The mob had been on the streets for hours; each target was some distance from the next. Mohammed's residence was nearly at the end of the mob's rampaging zone. They arrived, surrounded the modest bungalow, hacked Bala to death, and set fire to the house. The police had, of course, been long alerted, and Mohammed's error was his confidence that the police, who had long been on the streets in full force, would put an end to the mayhem in no time at all. How was he, or anyone not actually on the streets, to know that any time the police came upon the mob, they accompanied them some distance, then disappeared as the mob was about to mount an operation, and returned to accompany them to the next target—sometimes, just for variation, veering away in their personnel carriers as they came upon the crowd, then taking a long route round the town to rejoin them in time to make a show of dispersing them, after the mob had completed their deadly task. So Mohammed remained at home where he thought that his safety was assured.

The usual commission of enquiry was set up by the Kano state governor to assess the police peacekeeping conduct on that day. I ought to mention, by the way, that Kano was an opposition state to the supposedly democratic federal government of Shehu Shagari—which of course controlled the police. Why, the police commissioner was asked, had he failed to take strong action against the crowd? Most Nigerians still cite variations of that officer's response even in the most inapposite circumstances. His reply was: "because the mob was cooperative."

I feel compelled to recall this piece of democratic history because the "cooperative mob" has become quite a barometer of government cynicism, and its instrument of policy implementation, though "execution" would actually be a more accurate expression in recent times. How else to describe the conduct of the police in recent cases of religious riots in Northern Nigeria where the mob has been largely left to wreak destruction on perceived infidels at the slightest suggestion of a contrived or imagined provocation. The past two decades of Nigerian history have witnessed an unprecedented rash of so-called religious riots that have resulted in hundreds of deaths, many such riots being permitted to rage freely, with government forces either looking on, or being conspicuously absent. The fatuous commissions of enquiry that follow have become a substitute for prevention or control, warnings and distinct signs always being studiously ignored in advance. The commissions must not, of course, be considered totally without purpose; they tend to be highly motivated where there are political dissidents who can be implicated, however implausibly. And governmental alacrity in responding to these situations actually attains commendable levels whenever the victim group indicates that it has had enough, mobilizes, and strikes back. Then it is not only the armed police, hitherto absent, who suddenly flood the battle zone, but units of the army itself. This was the case with the religious riots of Kano in 1991 where the primary, perennial targets of Islamic extremists, the Igbo traders, unleashed a fierce counterattack on their tormentors. After that unexpected reverse for the cooperative mob, the police command underwent a virtual galvanization in its sense of peacekeeping. It moved to recall all licensed shotguns and hunting rifles in the entire country, under the pretext of curbing the epidemic of armed robbery!

Quantitatively speaking, however, the latest outrage of this nature was minuscule—one casualty only—in comparison with others, but the very individual nature of that execution possessed a kind of chilling clarity that the mass killings had lacked, exposing as it did a society being deliberately pitted against itself, again not so much by the act but by the studied indifference of a supposedly neutral umbrella of public security.

The causes remain, as usual, murky. Some claimed that the victim had insulted the Koran, others that he had mocked the religion, yet others that he had defiled the name of Mohammed, and so on and so on. Let no one miss the point: what happens in Turkey or Pakistan infects susceptible mentalities in far-off Nigeria; the case of one Taslima Nasreen does not end with her salvation in distant Sweden, and the attitude of the rest of the global community has a role to play in awakening governments to their responsibilities. Benazir Bhutto has at least displayed the expected courage, despite her clear disadvantage as a female leader in a society dominated by a male theocracy. The universally acknowledged but deliberately suppressed truth is that religious extremism is a malignant fungus that not only attacks weak tissues but casts its spores worldwide, encouraging emulation in its benign relations, even origins, by denigrating their innate pacifism as enfeeblement.

But let us return to our latest Nigerian scenario, barely a month old. The mob, instigated by their imam, went after the alleged culprit, broke down the gates to the prison where he had been given sanctuary, beheaded him, stuck his head on a spear and danced through the streets to the mosque where the imam preached a panegyric on their action. Again the attack took place in broad daylight, without one arrest, word of condemnation, threat, or response by any government agency. Not until days later when havoc was cried by some newspapers did the administration so much as remark that anything disturbing had taken place; then it commenced the usual lackadaisical motions in the direction of outrage.

It is my suspicion that the world at large is playing the game of the cooperative mob, or variants of the same theme, with one of the greatest plagues that has ever befallen humankind. Cooperation takes various forms naturally, the most familiar of which is continuing economic cooperation with states that actively breed, train, and finance the puppeteers of the "many-headed multitudes." The short-term policies of governments in global alliances have been equally responsible for this lethal phenomenon of chickens that have come home to roost, to the permanent discomfiture of their erstwhile financiers. The cooperative mob, we may observe, is not always a mob in the tumultuous sense, but can be an expression of mob conditioning, mob tyranny, the cowardice (called safety) in numbers, even where the numbers are physically absent and the act appears individual. That mob is the execution arm of the terminal censor. I see no difference, for instance, in the mentality of the mob collectivity that was programmed to slaughter young Mohammed, and the serial, individuated "mob" that has been responsible for the deaths of a hundred journalists, professors, doctors, artists, writers, and women (for the crime of being women) in Algeria and other parts of North Africa. I discern no difference between them and the mob that howl like jackals at full moon outside the abortion clinics of the United States, mobs who have succeeded in driving underground what is even now, however much resented, a legitimate practice, escalating a rhetoric of hate until it produces the desired result—terminal censorship. And I tend toward a feeling that the dominant perception of the world in relation to this phenomenon is one of a mildly delinquent mob whose assault against our humanity can somehow be indulged, or accommodated, because they are "cooperative" in some form or another.

Well, maybe not exactly. Shall we simply say, the misunderstood mob? The more-sinned-against-than-sinning mob? When Jimmy Carter said, of the Serbian butchers—whose victims, let us recall by the way, were and still are mostly made up of the Muslim population—when that peacemaker said that the Serbian leaders had been largely misunderstood, I could not understand the seeming reaction of outrage. I would have thought that he was merely employing the fin-de-siècle language of accommodation. The Serbs, who had, after all, contributed the most memorable, indeed, landmark phrase to the inhuman lexicon of this millennial ending, were merely being recompensed. Their concentration camps were a mere matter of misunderstanding, their rape of Muslim women, their use of civilian hostages for mine-clearing and forced labor—all, all, were a mere misunderstanding. It was the world that had failed an intelligence test, the world that failed to recognize that, since as individuals we all occasionally require a bath and a delousing, the racial or religious collectivity should be afforded the same hygienic facilities.

However, is it really that wide a gulf between the assurance that comes of being pronounced "misunderstood," and the induced empathy for any further acts of violation against the victims of the misunderstood? In any case, Jimmy Carter certainly left with the euphoric feeling that the Serbs had proved very cooperative! My intention, let me hasten to add, is not to belittle Carter's efforts toward global conflict resolution. On the contrary, the world could do with more such vigorous individual commitments. We can hardly ignore, however, the dangers posed by a conflation of good intentions with what amounts to a verbal cleansing of a gruesome reality.

To situate these concerns in graphic terms, we shall shortly peek in through the windows of some two or three habitations. They are all around us, and will, in all probability, expand and engulf us soon enough, physically or vicariously. Some of this audience might be tempted to protest that "it could never happen here," not within the serenity of these walls and the sanctuary of learning. But, if you will allow me to descend to some territory of lunacy for a moment, do explain to me how some products of such a system can actually prove capable of sending off letter bombs to members of a hunting fraternity, setting off explosions in homes, dynamiting animal farms, and so on, simply because of a love of the animal world. Fanaticism is an omnivore of multiple causes. It is not a question of whether or not the true destiny of humanity is to be vegetarian, or an idle set of English gentry should be much more usefully employed than to dress up in red velvet and breeches to chase a miserable fox over stiles and brooks only to surrender the quarry, in the end, to the slavering jaws of hunting hounds. Our extract here from these competitive absurdities is the murderous purism that leads to the formation of what we can only describe as parodies of civil resistance cells, on behalf of the dumb species, which engage in guerrilla action that accepts the crippling and even elimination of their own species as legitimate rules of combat on behalf of the defenseless fox or—the latest I have heard of—violent sabotage of the more contemplative preoccupation of the angler!

But to return to the more substantial cousins of the terminating imperative: "mindset" is one of those faddish expressions to which I react negatively, for some reason, but I find that, in looking for the common denominator between various manifestations of fundamentalist thought and self-righteous arrogation of terminal censorship against all unbelievers, we are returned time and time again to the territory of the human psyche that promotes the unintended accuracy of this expression. It is a useful, infinitely expandable phrasing. The mindset that must preoccupy us is never the resetting of your watch as you enter a new time zone. No, that watch is set permanently in the dark ages, in the dark corners of the mind, the darkest ages of superstition, the home of phantoms, of the terror of the unknown, the cringing fear of every new experience that leads to aggression, elimination, in order to conserve the static assurance of existence and the stunting of intellectual curiosity. It is the setting of the mind not on questions but on the mantra "I am right, you are wrong," of which the next stage of unreason is "I am right, you are dead!" It is not setting as being all set to go, to explore, since this implies motion, a sense of preparation for a voyage of discovery. This mindset is set as cement sets, as tar sets, as plaster of paris sets, as molten lava eventually sets along its path of devastation. It is set as setting the world on fire and probably as it wills that the sun should set permanently on humanity.

How does one explain this mindset? Or perhaps we should stick to the easier task: how does one explain its increasing prevalence, its increasing toleration? Apart from the familiar phenomenon of fear, of surrender through a deliberately cultivated unawareness, of hoping, silently, that the menace will eat itself up, collapse of its own untenability, that it will go away if simply ignored, are there perhaps other, far more active means of collaboration? I know of one, and it is that which constitutes my concern today. An "understanding" attitude toward far-reaching causes is a very ready tool in the accommodation of present evil, especially one that threatens the very existence of any active protester. That understanding often finds recourse in history, in the slights of history inflicted by external forces on whom, presumably, vengeance is now being wreaked. This is a lie, a ploy by which we are seduced into shrugging off the massacre of the entire Hindu or Muslim inhabitants of a village—not omitting their livestock—by the simple act of recollecting some antecedents. Such an example, however unnecessarily, expands the field of censorship with which I am concerned today; I cite it only as a logical extension, the need to recognize where such thinking leads. I am far more interested in those instances where history is used to justify even the contemporary victimization of those who are an integral part of the shared victim status of their new oppressors. Those victims who are manifestly, abundantly within that same history of external wrong. They are, in short, permanent victims of the murderous arrogance of their own kind, victims of a messianic impudence that denies them the reparations that are claimed by the self-proclaimed champions of their shared history, champions that indeed extract such reparations primarily from them, usually in blood or disfigurement, condemning them, in short, to an unjust existence of double jeopardy.

To offer a variation of the familiar folk tale of the hyena and the python, imagine that the hyena, who accused the python's ancestors of polluting the waters of his drinking hole by thrashing in it, now dedicates his life to savaging not only every serpentine creature and object in his path, but his own kith and kin, on the grounds that they have found a way of making water from that hole potable, instead of dying of thirst.

We are concerned, unavoidably, with the ongoing infliction of brutal injustice that appears to be the portion of victims of a particular history. Similarly, we are trying to understand also why one sector of the designated victim grouping links itself with the conduct of those real or presumed oppressors, acting against its own kind with identical impulses of hubris, transforming its minority existence into a new oppressor class against its own kind, and against the rest of humanity. Is this phenomenon entirely within the psychological terrain? Politics and history are clearly not sufficient. Sociology may help, and psychology is a stout contender. We, the laypeople who are, or who identify with, daily and potential victims, can only challenge certitudes by recalling the reels of reality over and over again, in fast forward and slow motion, in order to question the findings of pundits on their analytical but nonremedial perches. If there is immediate lack of a common causative denominator between the profiles of two subjects perpetrating an identical act that affects the well-being of humanity, two subjects widely separated in history and sociology, then we are compelled to continue our search beyond familiar parameters. If after this we are confronted by failure, that is, we are surely left with no option but to evolve independent strategies for our own self-protection. So let us return to our interrupted peeping-tom exercise and, peering through two widely separated windows, review certain actualities that are surely still freshly retained even in the most disinterested memory.

In a comfortable living room—free from the privations of millions of others, his contemporaries in other cultures who eke out a hardy existence in a dingy, disease-ridden, possibly overpopulated corner of the developing world—a young man sits and plots. He is gainfully employed, but if he is not, he is economically cushioned by the welfare state structures that guarantee a modest existence. Certainly he is not starved, and he is well clothed. Undoubtedly there is a television set in the living room, a refrigerator, maybe a small shelf of books. The well-nourished exterior of this man, however, belies an interior of discontent. A divine misanthropy engages his mind, a rage that will be translated into no less than a mission of divine retribution. Before him lies a gun, loaded, or an incendiary device. He awaits the moment for which he is sublimely primed.

Four thousand miles away from him, surrounded by half-starved siblings and other members of an extended family, sits one of those earlier contrasted contemporaries of our first subject. He is of a different race, is differently clothed, is certainly less educated in the Western understanding of that expression—and indeed even within the parameters of his own system of knowledge. But he is also full of righteous rage, an equally holy commitment. A woman, a man, has been pointed out to him as one who has dared challenge, in word or deed, the holy writ. He touches the handle of the dagger beneath his ragged robes and waits to cover himself in glory as a soldier of the supreme deity. He accepts the guidance and authority only of his holy mentor who, in comparative economic terms, may be equated with our first model, the Western individual whom we encountered in a centrally heated or air-conditioned flat, also awaiting his appointment with destiny.

That first, fired by the zeal of a holy crusade, will proceed to a medical clinic in a secluded suburb of the United States and open fire on a crowd, or a doctor, his staff, or patient. He will make his escape and proceed to stalk the next victim on his list. These establishments are guilty of disobeying his beloved scriptures which, in his reading, forbid the act of abortion. The sacrosanct commandment, "Thou shalt not kill," sums up the fundamentals of his obsession. This sanctity of life he will proceed to defend with the extinction of other lives, yet this zeal, this deadly contradiction, remains to him both real and pure. And this, his act, is also not a lone one. Even if, unlike his counterpart in North Africa, Pakistan, India, or Turkey, the act has not been ordered, or is not proved to have been ordered, it receives instant jubilation among his kind. He is named a martyr to the cause, and is assured of a place in the Christian paradise. Indeed, a fellow believer will pronounce, without a tinge of irony, without a sense of the macabre, the following chilling judgment on his action: "There's nothing wrong with John whatsoever, other than he killed a couple of people."

And from the lips of yet another proselyte of the same religious fervor, the definitive judgment: "They are worrying about two or three people dead when millions of unborn lives have already been snuffed out by these same people."

The mental sibling of both, on the other side of the globe, will stalk a journalist whose writings have offended his mentor, or a woman whose conduct, perhaps just a mode of dressing, has offended the injunctions, in the view of that divine intermediary, of the Holy Word. He will stab one to death, stone or behead the other. The woman is especially prone to a vicious death because it is not just she as an individual but her entire sex that is guilty. The scriptures, as pronounced by this young man's mentor and minder, appear to be tailored primarily for the circumscription of her place in society. To flout such a reading in any way is to challenge the divine order of the world.

The journalists on their part are lewd purveyors of alien values. They promote the woman's struggle for dignity as an equal member of the human race. They are tempters who reveal alternatives and values, and they are considered frontline enemies because they possess, as do other writers, an armory of unholy words in which to extract and rephrase, for the purposes of demystification, passages from those same scriptures that contest the divine doctrine of female subservience and male domination. Passages, in general, that challenge the sole authority of the fatal interpreter of the divine word. But it is not the journalists and writers alone who find themselves gravely at risk. Other priests whose reading of the holy book lacks the desired homicidal zeal are equally marked down for elimination. The only test, it seems, for authenticity in the reading of the holy scriptures is the ability to order deaths or mutilation, or to condone them.

Ambitiously, the prelate also aims for bigger prey. He needs to demonstrate that his law, his interpretation of the divine law, respects no one, however highly placed or eminently regarded both within and without his national borders. And so this executioner of the divine will punctiliously identify the handiwork of other unholy scribblers, proceeds to strike down a Naguib Mahfouz to serve as a lesson to others, issues a *fatwa* against a Taslima Nasreen and hounds her out of her homeland.

How reassuring the intent must be adjudged, even where such consolation is dismally disproportionate to the havoc that provoked it, when we learn sometimes that a brutal assault on our humane sensibilities is the act of one deranged individual, not the result of a conspiracy by many, not the project of a group dementia. Thus a crumb of consolation was extracted from the fact that the Israeli reservist who opened fire on Muslim worshippers in a mosque in Jerusalem appeared to have acted alone. But did he indeed act alone? Even if the revelations that came later, indicting the military command of criminal laxity, of discriminatory codes of engagement that definitely encouraged such a massacre, had never been made, the truth is that this outrage, the handiwork of a fanatic hand, was not the product of a lone ranger. We insist, in other words, that such minds are numerous, such obsessive hatred for the other exists in tens, if not hundreds, of thousands of minds and only awaits the triggering moment, the reward of nurturing consciousness of societal approval, overt or covert, telltale signals of official dereliction—a policy of discrimination and graded citizenship—to turn a private fantasy into a universal nightmare.

And so, to the other two fatal models of intolerance, we add that picture, fleshed out in the inevitable postmortem on a preventable catastrophe, of a mind that obviously claims to be in direct communication with some supreme deity. To him, the pious chants of Muslims in their rites of worship constitute a desecration of spiritual purity that must be exorcised, brutally and terminally.

If only indeed he had acted alone, but, we insist, he did

not! He did not act alone because—he is not alone. Every assault on our humanity by the fanatic mind is the consequence of a societal complicity that goes back in our various histories and often extends beyond national borders. Thus, we must begin to address such aberrant conduct in universal terms. An evil protagonist has merely played out the rules that evolve naturally from abandonment of a collective responsibility, the worst aspect of which is a manifest helplessness that makes one an accessory before the fact, for these signs are usually omnipresent; a docility of will and collective dereliction lead inevitably to our tragic discomfiture.

Since the beginning of the articulated word, a need appears to have evolved for some kind of categorization that would set one word a world apart—indeed worlds, even an entire universe apart—from the next. It would be extremely instructive to find out how this came about. In thinking of oral cultures, or shall we say, considering those cultures that still preserve oral exposition as part of their way of life, quite outside routine communication, we do find examples of dangers posed to a community through wrongful recitation of some liturgy or incantation. Even where a specific passage is so obscure that no one can proffer a literal meaning for it, an error in the order of recital may indeed be held to portend dire consequences for the individual or the society, requiring some rites of cleansing or appeasement to ward off the calamity. Except in fairy tales or opera, however—the suitor must interpret a riddle, complete a proverb thereby winning the hand of a princess or losing his head—I know of no example in oral culture that prescribes a mandatory capital punishment for a real or imagined crime against a divine text. Is this perhaps a long unsuspected lethal property of the written word that erupts from time to time, like a dormant virus or volcano? Christianity and Islam appear to be the most vulnerable to such destructive traits. Maybe it is time we devoted some serious global attention to why, throughout the ages, the mere materialization, on perishable parchment or paper, even stone, of some immutably determined word, evokes such mortal and primitive passions. It all centers on power and domination, of course, of which the written word is mystic weapon, the magic amulet of terrestially ambitious priesthood—but that belongs in another province of its own, requiring its own exposition in depth.

During the Nigerian civil war, when the federal troops overran the university town of Nsukka, the report was that they made first for the university library, where they proceeded to rip out the pages of books, and use them to light fires or as toilet paper. There was no shortage of firewood in Nsukka, and I believe there must have been masses of old newspaper, which one might consider far more suitable for that latter purpose.

The battleground is, of course, the mind. Those of us whose entire lives appear to have been spent in contesting the inhumanities and arrogance of state, who constantly denounce and place ourselves at risk before the monstrosities that constitute and manifest themselves as the very being and essence of the state, find ourselves compelled today to turn our concern and anger against the unstructured, arbitrary, indeed amorphous bid for the territory of power by the fanatic surge that appears resolved to usher us into the next century. The evidence has been long with us. In February 1987, at a Paris meeting of Nobel laureates initiated by Elie Wiesel and hosted by President François Mitterand, I drew attention to the signs of a new authoritarianism of the fanatic brand that appeared to have sniffed a vacuum in the collapse of communism. It seemed to be rushing to proclaim itself heir to the strain of violent domination in localized and global interaction, resolved to operate by coercion, despising reason and discourse. A few months later, the first *fatwa* to attain the proportions of an international challenge, and to extend the claims of both spiritual and secular authority to a universal, terminal censorship of ideas and imagination, was issued against the writer Salman Rushdie.

Since that precedent, a rash of mimic competitors, no less deadly in intent, has erupted all around the globe to serve terminal notice on all, of whatever religion or ideological persuasion, who insist on exercising their faculties of intellect, imagination, exploration, and lifestyle in the most meaningful direction that their creative enlargement can conceive of.

The preceding selection of scenarios among thousands embracing a hundred or more faiths and their varied strains—Sikhs, Hindus, Jews, Shiites, Sunnis, scientologists, Moonies, Born Again and Right-to-Life Christians, and so on—surely cautions against reductionist approaches to the menace of the zealot, approaches that attempt to explain away such phenomena on purely historical or sociological grounds. These are only part of the story. The phenomenon of fanaticism involves environment, obviously, but it is largely a teaching, nurturing, indoctrinating environment, a process of formation to which the middle-class intellectual or businessperson may be just as vulnerable as the socially aggrieved product of a decaying ghetto. Most often it is a product, from any rung up or down the ladder of economic well-being and class structure, of power-driven minds: quite unscrupulous, usually modest in the commencing territorial ambition, but constantly alert and amenable to expansionist opportunities. That certain social conditions provide ideal breeding grounds for more susceptible human material is not in dispute, especially when the indoctrinating process can be linked to real or imagined social or historical injustices. Nonetheless, the fanatic, intolerant mind, to be effectively countered, must first be addressed as a self-inflicted, self-reproducing phenomenon. "Understanding" must be recognized as a two-way proceeding: if you want me to understand your existential absolute, you are obliged also to endeavor to understand mine. This is the foundation of a rational coexistence.

We must not imagine either that the crusader against the right of women to decide individual limitations on the weight of burden their bodies should bear will be content to restrict his or her activities to the confines of the United States. He will seek allies fired with an equally impeccable piety. Soon, even those who merely condemn such overweening arrogance will be categorized as unholy, disposable vermin, or—to use the diabolical shorthand of all such soldiers of the divine will—"legitimate targets." Thus, targeted by holy zeal, an editor of a libertarian journal in secular Switzerland will find himself the victim of a mysterious arson or, worse, encounter a hail of bullets as he clips on his skis in the quiet ski resort of Davos.

If I may be permitted the indulgence of citing myself as example, no sooner had an article I had written appeared in my own national newspaper, condemning the *fatwa* against Rushdie, than the students in one of our universities surged out into the streets carrying placards which decreed Death to Soyinka. Of a presumably loftier level of the homicidal instinct, the unctuous, sanctimonious variety, was a follow-up letter to the press whose author declared, in the most lugubrious, self-chiding, Uriah-Heepy tone, that he did not consider himself suffused with sufficient piety, else he would have himself, personally, placed a *fatwa* over the head of that same blasphemer. I tried to capture the persona of that specific correspondent in my mind. I imagined him as a young man of about twenty-four, turning steadily anorexic as he fasted round the clock to purify himself for the divine privilege of ordering yet another mental case to stalk Wole Soyinka, and stick a knife in his back. The saddest picture of all was the incongruity of the setting—a place of learning, a secular, university institution.

In Israel, a Jewish sect, let it not be forgotten, also affirmed the righteousness of the *fatwa* against Salman Rushdie, stopping short, I recall, of actually pronouncing a similar fate against the filmmaker Martin Scorcese for his *The Last Temptation of Christ*. And back to Nigeria once again, a keen sports writer, a Christian, well known also for his incisive excoriation of social ills, devoted his column at the time to a furious denunciation of the author of *The Satanic Verses* and the appropriateness of the death sentence imposed on him, indulging, indeed, in the most excruciating pun on Rushdie's name—Rush-die. Die, Rushdie, die, he declaimed. You deserve it, your name has marked you down, and die you must. By contrast, and to their eternal credit, let us note that the League of Muslim Imams from my part of Nigeria issued a no less strongly worded condemnation of the *fatwa*, indicting its annunciator for spiritual hubris and impiety. They were not alone. Various Islamic bodies throughout the world disputed the claims of Ayatollah Ruholla Khomeini to the custodianship of the sword of vengeance of Allah, declaring that the supreme deity was perfectly capable of defending his own name and sanctity.

Now, the significance of this opposition roll call should be retained in our minds when we come later to explore the role of the intelligentsia, of some persuasions at least, in the kind of revisionism that is creeping slowly over the terrain of academia. We need to probe the flabby tissues of their new language of accommodation as handmaiden to the territorial expansionism of our terminal censors.

I speak with the concern of one who could boast, some two decades ago, that his own nation was virtually free of this scourge. Not any longer. Not since the eruption, notably, of a fanatic sect called the Maitatsine, which claimed (like many others) to be the authentic torchbearers of Islam, but whose murderous hostility was primarily directed against other Muslims, against all and any Muslims of whatever sect. Nothing less than a military engagement, including aerial bombardment, succeeded in terminating the most brutal rampage of religious zealotry that the nation had ever known. With a racial-emotive battle cry raised against Mohammed as a false prophet and slaving Arab, Maitatsine reserved its most rabid contempt for blacks who dared acknowledge the "Arab" religion as theirs. It drew a large following from the lumpenproletariat, employed tactics of systematic intimidation to take over houses, then entire city quarters, until it had built itself a virtual stronghold within the state where vote-hunting politicians (incidentally also Muslim) came to bargain for its support. Even the earlier mentioned governor of Kano state, Abubakar Rimi, whose adviser fell to the orchestrated rampage of the original cooperative mob, considered Maitatsine so cooperative as to deserve more than one courtesy visit!

If only for the benefit of competitive custodians of ultimate truth, and the apologists of marshmallow cultural sensibilities, we are obliged to spend a few moments on this ill-reported event—ill reported in the outside world, that is. He, Maitatsine, was the awaited last prophet. He had the keys of paradise with him and, after his departure from earth and glorious entry into that afterlife pleasure resort, the gates of paradise would be firmly, eternally locked. All late arrivals had only one condition left to them—eternal torment! The nearest Christian equivalent I can recall, in the intensity of zealotry and blind faith, was the eruption of the Alice cult in Uganda. (Her followers included lawyers, university professors, and former diplomats and politicians.) Maitatsine's followers threw themselves on police guns with rapturous abandon, the difference from the Alice movement being that they did not consider themselves immune from the white man's bullets but courted them, mortally afraid for their souls' perdition if they failed to attain paradise before the anointed one. This one-eyed, and incidentally unprepossessing, individual operated a Jonestown-like domain.[4] He accumulated weapons and, with increasing boldness, raided railway trains in Northern stations, killed off the men, and kidnapped the women for use as sex and domestic slaves. His gospelling disdain and doomsday imprecations on the car-owning, "Westernized," affluent class—of whatever religion—was sufficient to fool the leftists. With a truly depressing predictability, they declared, from their theoretical sanctuaries, that this was the revolutionary messiah come to liberate the poor and the downtrodden.

When the military finally subdued the "revolutionary," the gory spectacle was revealed of a wide and deep charnel house within the stronghold where hundreds of murdered victims—usually strangled or bludgeoned to death—had been thrown. Nigerians could not credit the images that were presented by the media, on television, could not believe that these systematic atrocities had taken place within their own national borders, and in peacetime. Some had been killed straight after captivity—kidnapped at night, in broad daylight, on their farms, or from their homes—or later murdered for any infringements of the new holy writ. The handful of survivors spoke of a nightmare of existence, emerging traumatized for the rest of their lives. Quite a number of Maitatsine's followers were known to have escaped; their sporadic activities, whenever reported, still send tremors of destabilization through the populace. And since that evil watershed, how many other strains there have been, each competing with the last for escalating levels of savage conversion, for territorial aggrandizement within institutions, public policies, and private conduct!

Indeed, there is hunger, an enemy of human well-being that must be addressed. There is the inadequacy of shelter, the scourge of diseases, unequal distribution of resources and opportunity for social development. There is the continuing plague of those other tin gods, the obdurate despots, military and civilian, who persist in thwarting the democratic will of peoples all over the world. There will always be natural disasters, such as the recent devastation of Kobe in Japan, by earthquake, floods, and tornadoes, all of which the ingenuity

of man tries valiantly to anticipate and mitigate. And man-
made disasters of monumental scale, like Chechnya, Rwanda,
or Somalia. And the energies of the progressive world must
continue to be focused on these, to rid the world of both the
causes and the effects that continue to drag humanity down
in defiance of its manifest potential. I believe, however, that a
structured concern with the global menace of fanaticism has
become the emergent imperative of our times. What AIDS
has proved to be to the body, fanaticism is to the mind. The
millennial dream can only be that of tolerance and acceptance, of inclusion, not exclusion. Fanaticism is an implacable
enemy of that dream. The challenge that it poses must be
recognized, and accepted. The world must remain principled
but become equally obdurate in its response.

For a start, the language by which this infliction is
addressed must be amended in order to alter the state of consciousness by which we confront a common enemy. The
guilt-ridden euphemisms and effete phrase-mongering of so-
called "political correctness" must be abandoned in favor of
unambiguous terms of condemnation. I do not speak in the
abstract but from increasing encounters with the effect of language as an instrument of paralysis of individuals and communities of thought, a paralysis that goes beyond inaction,
since it now moves from mere withdrawal to a complicity
with the forces of repression, condemning action in others by
the assumption of a seemingly superior but simply perverse
theology of pseudocultural relativism.

Curiously, this compliance of language also operates in a
reverse form, through overkill and/or misdirection. A sense of
horror can be blunted simply by overloading the basket, placing
in the same quarantine cage-birds of totally different plumage.
A periodic affliction of society—a positive affliction, it must
be conceded—is that it does examine its own habits in the
light of new knowledge. One danger of having a checklist, in
which all questionable forms of conduct are moralistically

lumped, and given a tag of pejorative equivalence, is that the finer discriminatory senses are blunted, enabling what is clearly evil to obtain acceptance, or tolerance, or deferred action. In Yoruba, we say: *E fi ete sile, e npa lapalapa.* It means, roughly, you ignore the leprosy, and expend your energies on the common ringworm. Or again: the condemned prisoner takes his final walk into eternity and you ask him to spit out his cigarette because it might give him cancer. When I hear, for instance, cigarette smoking, or advertising described as— and I quote precisely here—"a crime against humanity," I know that an alibi for or attenuation of the authentic crimes against humanity is in the offing. One moment, in the midst of a conflict-resolution conference, you are justifiably in the heart of Yugoslavia and Rwanda, the next moment you find you have been transponded into Marlboro Country! What, I was inclined to mock, had become of the reigning fad of cultural sensitivity? Tobacco culture preexisted European imperialism, as Sir Walter Raleigh would have been happy to testify. Seriously, such unholy enthusiasm does a disservice to that very humanity by cheapening our sense of moral revulsion, leaving it sated by the time it encounters far more grievous atrocities. Not necessarily on its own, no, but it does contribute in a subterranean manner, becoming part of a negative progression, a cumulative erosion of the limited sensibilities for outrage of the average individual. What exactly is being proposed to our moral attunement when cigarette smoking is placed on the same level of moral damnation as the crime of genocide?

If we can find our way out of that smokescreen, we may discover that this hyperbolic strain can actually squeeze out the most basic information required to redress the world, or bits and pieces of it anyway, and I mean this in the most practical way. I tend to warn myself against the temptations of a conspiracy theory, so when the world media insist that the Angolan war is the longest running civil war in Africa, I put it down to ignorance, and the open internationalization of that war—apartheid to the south, Russia and America contending for the roles of angel and devil, and Cuba insisting on its disinterested solidarity of intervention. The truth, however, is that the Sudan has experienced, and is still undergoing, the longest running civil war on the continent, and arguably the most brutish. If only it were a mere mythification problem, a media sloppiness, with no consequences of both African and international neglect for the southern Sudanese as a long-suffering people, who remain victims of a virulent strain of theocratic tyranny!

Contemporary media language is, to restate the obvious, singularly potent, both for positive and negative ends. It can direct massive universal attention, just as in subtle, often unconscious, ways it can and does induce neglect, promote ignorance, divert attention away from crucial issues, and can indeed be held culpable for missed opportunities in ethical lessons. In the struggle for a democratic order on the continent, which is the same as saying in the struggle to make power and authority constantly accountable, no lesson can be considered too trivial, and when the little victories that result in drastic social changes place such opportunities in our way—monumental opportunities—it is very frustrating indeed that such occasions are not only not maximized, but are actually suppressed.

Two trials of immense significance are actually in progress on the African continent at this moment. One is the trial of the octogenarian, erstwhile president for life of Malawi, Hastings Kamuzu Banda, for conspiracy to murder and other abuses of power.[5] The other is of course that of the mass murderer and ideological torturer, the self-avowed Marxist Mariam Mengistu of Ethiopia.[6] The latter trial in particular is of a dimension that is little short of that of the Nuremberg trials.

These are trials that unborn children all over the world, and on the African continent especially, should learn about;

but we are more concerned about the living, the tortured, and the dying, and the possible amelioration of their condition, even their salvation, by placing such trials on the world stage, side by side perhaps with that of the Serbian president Slobodan Milosevic and his agents, with General Leopoldo Galtieri of Argentina probably thrown in for geographical spread. If, since we are living in a market-directed media trade, it is a question of drama, of dramatic interest, I cannot envisage the failure of the trial of Mariam Mengistu, at least, to rivet the attention of television addicts worldwide. What, instead, are we offered? What, indeed, is touted as "the trial of the century," into which the entire world has been assiduously programmed, like docile drug addicts? The tawdry, commonplace pseudo-drama of a faded football hero called O. J. Simpson. Even regular programs on the all-conquering CNN are shunted aside to give room for some latest "development" or action from a land whose very byword, whose very national imprint, is dialogue through violence! The trials of the century are taking place right now in the heart of Africa, and they are trials that serve as a moral and a warning both to surviving dictators and their international props of the left and the right. Media hype has, however, dictated other *foci*, and even the affluent of the African continent who can afford the satellite dish are besotted by this fare. My latest information is that cassettes are now available for sale of the thrilling episodes of this twentieth-century saga! Here, of course, we do have a direct correlation, albeit a negative one, between rhetoric and impact. What is lost or suppressed is unnoticed, and thus its potential is wasted. With such powerful injections of lowlife self-indulgence, is it any wonder that a neopuritanism asserts itself in other spheres as some instinctive talisman of self-protection?

To return to the verbal mechanics of ethical manipulation, however, no concept that I know of comes close in hypodermic phrase-mongering to that profane phraseology known as political correctness! There appears to be no abyss of mindlessness, no social absurdity, no intellectual shame, or ideological flatulence to which this baggage will not aspire— that much I had accepted already—yet even I had to catch my breath with disbelief when, on a university campus in Canada, I encountered the prevailing view that it was now "politically incorrect" to speak out on behalf of Salman Rushdie! It was not simply sections of the university but, from all appearances, quite a sizeable portion of the intellectual and artistic community in Toronto that could be deemed to have succumbed to this creed. I am convinced, of course, that there is some exaggeration in my perception, but during my entire stay of a week of lectures, seminars, media interviews, and interaction with writers and artists in their watering holes, this special community of thought and creativity appeared to be divided into two: a minority of notional sophisticates that espoused such a view with nothing short of religious fervor, and the rest, who had been cowed into submission. Hovering around the two groups floated the vocal storm troopers of certain minority causes, clear-sighted, opportunistic, and cynical. Their agenda was strictly limited: to exploit the moral confusion and social guilt that had been implanted in the community and thus obtain the maximum social benefits from such a situation for themselves and their causes. That, at least, I could understand and, frankly, applaud.

Ironically, Rushdie was himself making his first public appearance in a different part of Canada, Ottawa, in the company of the prime minister. I was in Toronto, being honored, and again, by a coincidence, an institute of Islamic studies had just boosted the price on the head of Salman Rushdie by a million dollars. Since mine was an academic occasion, it seemed to me only appropriate that I should utilize my own space of scholarship to rebuke that institution, insisting that the cause of learning in any field cannot be served through censorship, especially of the terminal kind. Indeed, I offered the other side—not for the first time, I should add—what I considered a solution in the true spirit of scholarship and, since this was their major concern, religious dedication. Perhaps I should state it again—who knows, the idea might eventually catch on.

It is a simple one really: since ink it was that gave the offense, ink should be made to provide the remedy. In short, I challenged the institute—I have forgotten its exact name— as well as the original Iranian Murder Incorporated—to offer a fraction of the proposed blood-money to a select consortium of writers (myself included, naturally) who would together produce the most exemplary text of the life of the prophet Mohammed ever written. Imagine the product of a collaboration between poet and historian, theologian and epic novelist—or indeed allied combinations! If such a work fails to become a universal bestseller, then the critics should be shot—they should accept that they have a crucial role to play in this, after all. In my part of the world, this would be considered a humane and ennobling recompense, a project of spiritual reconciliation, one that is faithful to the word of Islam which stands, above all, for peace.

Afterward I received the usual pats on the back—for what I thought was some creative, original thinking. But the word that kept cropping up was "courageous." Now that had me baffled. Every professor, student, or visitor who offered commentary stressed this word, and with such feeling that I wondered if the police had spotted some dacoits lurking around the convocation hall looking for Salman Rushdie. But Rushdie was in Ottawa, not Toronto, and hopefully I would have made my escape by the time they learned that there was a Nigerian around who dared to condemn their odious mission.

It was not until dinner afterward that I learned exactly against whom this "courage" was understood to have had been directed. It was not in the direction of the would-be killers but against the new orthodoxy that had taken over the community and held it captive. The origins, as usual, were murky, but clearly Rushdie had become part of some other forms of cultural contestations; in the process, it was suddenly (or progressively) discovered that Salman Rushdie had not been sensible to the cultural feelings of others, therefore it was politically incorrect that his cause should be espoused! I had apparently taken on, innocently, the new commissars of thought whose domination, in that area of intellectual exchange at least, had become total. This was the unholiest cut of all.

One (white) professor was particularly effusive in his gratitude for my David versus Goliath act, which, he confessed, he had longed to undertake but felt clearly disadvantaged about on account of his race.

Inside my head, the questions tumbled over one another, absurd scenarios and melodramatic variations. Salman Rushdie somehow separated from his minders in Ottawa, hotly pursued by his dogged would-be assassins, dodges in and out of campus alleyways, hides, they run past him, he dashes to a house that seems isolated and safe, knocks on the door, pleading sanctuary. A head pops out, recognizes the face and screams at him, "Go away! This is a politically correct house." Fugitive dashes to the staff common room, is met at the door by a smiling doctor of philosophy. "Ah, Salman, just wait outside while I phone the dean to find out what is the politically correct course of action." And so on, and on.

I had always thought that murder is murder, and incitement to murder a cowardly complicity in the act of murder. As Langston Hughes wrote, "There is no lavender word for 'lynch,'"[7] and acquiescence in any form, in the progression toward a lynching is, within any community, the commencement of the collapse of all human values within that community. In the intellectual community in particular, it is the end of its very reason for existence. For the global community, there is only one question: Do we all now submit to lynch law?

In a world where a near-octogenarian, Naguib Mahfouz, a creative giant in any community, but so rooted to his own that he hardly ever leaves it physically, in any world where such a prolific being can be stabbed at the instigation of a band of zealots, it should be clear to all that humanity is on trial, and that sociological excuses are surely as banal as the language of political correctness, crossing the border between impotence and complicity. In a situation where journalists write their own obituaries, knowing full well that each day may be their last, those who are outside the zone of terror have at least a fundamental obligation not to trivialize language in addressing their plight. We must go further, we must move into the territory of political will, move even from rhetorical denunciation to political strategies. The breeding grounds of fanaticism need to be sterilized and their insatiable gullet economically starved. Nations must come together, remove their diplomatic blinkers, and act in concert. The universal peril of fanaticism must, at one level or the other, become a priority project of the United Nations—a beginning has been made by designating this year as the Year of Tolerance. The Arab nations have recognized that they are especially imperiled, and have taken the lead at a special summit to address the menace. Their efforts must be reinforced by the rest of the world, and largely through preemptive strategies.

Because revelation is privileged and exclusive, its ramifications cannot be held to be universal, and its incursions into civic society can only be through persuasion and consent. By contrast, humanity is the one universal reality that can be apprehended both subjectively and objectively. It is that humanity that makes up society, and any social project, to have validity, can only be based on properties of that apprehended humanity. Intuitions and revelations, which become structured into faiths and religions, can only remain affairs of private conviction, although we are all free to join in acts and observances of their celebration.

The twenty-first century world that we envisage will clearly not be a universe of secular nations—more is the pity—but the sentient beings that people it can only cohabit through secular arbitrations. That much, I hope, is incontestable. Only this secular order of negotiations, because it is universal, can guarantee and enhance those privileged areas of spiritual intuitions as they impinge upon the rest of us, who are not so privileged and make no pretense of being on a first-name relationship with the divine mind with which, surely, the fanatic mind can be held to be in competition.

That, however, is again within the realms of supposition, and thus, superstition. If I choose to believe that the fanatic mind is in direct competition with the omnipotence and omniscience of divine being, and is thus deserving of divine retribution, that can only be regarded as a biased extension of my reverence for the unique repletion of that same divinity. I would be claiming, in short, that, being unknowable by definition, any mortal authoritative presumption as to His intentions is a sin, and therefore deserving of punishment. Since, however, my deductions are based on pure intuition and are therefore every bit as valid or invalid as my next-door neighbor's, I cannot justify my taking up an ax in the name of the unknowable and sinking it into that neighbor's head for his own convictions, any more than I could permit him to do the same to me. It then becomes the duty of the state—the commonly shared structure of civic existence—to prevent such a potential state of anomie while guaranteeing both of us the right to enshrine our individual intuitions in organized observances that are independent of, or may embrace, each other's. The alternative to this is a will to domination, exercised through intimidation, terror, and violence. This is the reality that confronts us in many parts of the world, demanding, for our mortal survival, a crucial revision of our posture toward that rampaging other, that supremacist, intolerant other, that fascistic, apocalyptic other who will sooner erase the world than share its potential for yet unsuspected routes to universal enlightenment. We must consciously devise means of rehabilitating this fanatic mind, luring it into the embrace of the universal shrine of humanity whose portals are ever wide open. Beyond them, we may glimpse the enticing vistas that the creative—and optimistic—mind has been spared to project into the next millennium.

GAY AUTOFICTION: THE SACRED AND THE REAL

Edmund White

Gay liberation began in 1969 with the Stonewall Uprising in New York, but it did not produce a significant literature for another ten years. To be sure, essayists (Hocquenghem in France, Tripp in America, Altman in Australia)[1] had begun in the early seventies to write theoretical works about homosexuality, but fiction had to wait until 1978 to make a major impact.[2]

At that time a new gay fiction emerged, which is still flourishing today. The defining characteristics of this fiction are that it is unapologetic, that it is addressed primarily to gay rather than straight readers, and that it conceives of homosexuality as an oppressed minority group rather than as a pathology. Less theoretically, this new fiction has commandeered new bookstores, new publishing houses, and even new magazines to review it. In New York, where the phenomenon is at its most advanced, an organization of gay people in publishing counts several hundred members and hands out an important literary prize every year.[3] In universities around the United States there are departments of queer studies; Harvard publishes a gay and lesbian review; the Beinecke library at Yale houses an important collection of contemporary gay and lesbian literary archives; the Center for Lesbian and Gay Studies at City University of New York, headed by Martin Duberman,[4] the celebrated historian, has become a bastion of this dynamic new movement, but Duke University is also celebrated for its department of queer studies, headed by the redoubtable Eve Kosofsky Sedgwick.[5]

Lesbian fiction has from the very beginning been associated in the United States with the feminist movement, except when it was entirely separatist. Only a few lesbian novelists—Jeanette Winterson in Great Britain,[6] Rita Mae Brown in the United States[7]—have become "crossover" writers with a mass-market audience including, presumably, many straight readers. Perhaps a few more gay male writers—Paul Monette,[8]

David Leavitt,[9] and Armistead Maupin[10] in the United States, Alan Hollinghurst,[11] Paul Bailey,[12] and Adam Mars-Jones[13] in England—enjoy this crossover status.

International comparisons, however, can be misleading, since they disguise the very different ways in which each country is culturally organized and politically structured. In Germany, where no major self-identified gay writer has emerged in the twenty years since the death of Hubert Fichte,[14] gay fiction is considered to be little better than a joke, usually a dirty one; there may or may not be a more pronounced homophobia in Germany than in other European countries, but I suspect the differences are more reasonably attributed to the fortuitous absence of "out" gay novelists of the first rank. When the brilliant Rainer Werner Fassbinder was alive, for instance, and Werner Schroeter was more active, one could have spoken of a distinguished gay German cinema, despite Fassbinder's lack of interest in male homosexuality as a subject (*Fox and His Friends* is his only gay film about men).

France represents a different social configuration. There are many outstanding gay writers—Dominique Fernandez, Tony Duvert, Renaud Camus,[15] as well as several who have died in the last decade, such as Hervé Guibert, Guy Hocquenghem, and Gilles Barbedette[16]—but I'm sure none of these writers except possibly the militant Fernandez would accept the label "gay writer," although all of them have written primarily about aspects of their own sexual identity. I don't even bother here with those numerous writers such as Angelo Rinaldi and Hector Bianciotti who write only occasionally if quite convincingly about homosexuality.[17]

What is striking is that none of these writers, not even those most concerned with gay content, was willing to attend an international congress of lesbian and gay writers held in London some years ago; in fact all of them, with the exception of the lesbian poet Geneviève Pastre,[18] responded angrily

to the invitation and denounced the ghettoization of literature, which the French contingent conceived of as a loss of
freedom. Whereas most English-language writers perceive the
evolution of openly gay fiction as progressive, in France the
same label is treated contemptuously as reactionary and belittling. Nor can the French attitude be dismissed as closeted-
ness or as a case of "Latin" *bellafigurismo,*[19] since in Italy, at
least, gay writers such as Pier Vittorio Tondelli and Aldo
Busi[20] have gladly accepted the label.

No, France is a country in which at least the illusion is
maintained of an open, civilized communication among all
the elements of society; the strong push toward secularism, at
least as old as the Revolution, has always militated against
special interest groups of any sort, whether religious or ethnic; literature and the "genius of the French language" have
been defined at least for three centuries as universal. In
France there is no black novel, no Jewish novel, and certainly
no gay novel, although a black Caribbean writer such as
Patrick Chamoiseau can win the Goncourt,[21] and many
French writers have been Jewish or homosexual or both.

In Britain the situation seems to be located somewhere
between the extremes represented by the United States and
France. High culture in general and gay culture in particular
enjoy more visibility in the United Kingdom than in the
United States; it was British television, after all, that made a
series out of Maupin's *Tales of the City,* that featured my own
biography of Jean Genet on a "South Bank Show," and did a
filmed version of Jeanette Winterson's *Oranges Are Not the
Only Fruit*; now British television is filming Hollinghurst's
The Swimming Pool Library. American television would never
initiate such programs, and even these British productions are
replayed in the United States after midnight and only on
obscure cable channels with names such as "Bravo." This
American invisibility will become still more marked given the
current political climate and the Republicans' hostility toward

National Public Radio and public television, not to mention homosexuality—virtually the only common enemy hated by all the disparate elements making up the right now that communism has vanished.

In Britain an out gay writer, Adam Mars-Jones, can be named the film critic of a national newspaper and another gay novelist, Alan Hollinghurst, can be the deputy editor of the leading literary journal and be nominated for the Booker Prize. I suppose it is symptomatic of British attitudes that *The Folding Star* would be classified by Waterstone's both on the shelf for literary fiction and on the shelf for gay fiction. In France no bookstore would have a shelf for gay fiction and in America no gay novel could be classed with general literary fiction or, as the shelf is now labelled in the United States, "Proven Authors."

The ghettoization of gay literature in the English-speaking world—and the refusal of France to acknowledge the very existence of gay fiction—have been two equally effective if opposite strategies for disguising the fact that gay literature does exist and that it has been central to the evolution of "autofiction," one of the main tendencies in continental literature. All too often, even when sophisticated English-speaking critics discuss French fiction, for instance, those works that are labelled "gay" are the minor ones, whereas the truth is that a great twentieth-century tradition in France is based on autobiographical fiction by gay men who have written at least to a substantial degree about their gay experience. I'm thinking of Marcel Proust, André Gide, Jean Cocteau, Marcel Jouhandeau, and, in our own day, Hervé Guibert and Tony Duvert.

Perhaps because I live in Paris I can already imagine the outraged whispers. I can recall that when I was working on my biography of Genet, my French publisher (and Genet's), Gallimard, was terribly worried that I'd turn my subject into a "gay writer." This fear arose not only from my reputation as an apologist but also because in conversation I'd once casually referred to Rimbaud as a "gay poet," which had profoundly shocked my editor.

Whereas I can understand the French reluctance to quarantine literature—a position I sympathize with in some ways on certain days—I cannot tolerate the reflex that bans all references to homosexuality while discussing a writer such as Genet, who wrote four autobiographical novels in which the narrator and protagonist, named "Jean Genet," presents his homosexual experiences in great detail to the reader, a reader who is explicitly designated as heterosexual. (Curiously, only in *Querelle*, the one wholly invented novel, is the reader imagined to be homosexual.)[22] As I tried to show in my biography, an impressive part of Genet's originality lies in his positioning of himself and the reader with regard to homosexuality, which he called his "jewel" and counted among his three cardinal virtues, along with theft and betrayal.

At a time when most middle-class gay writers were projecting their sexual orientation on fictional characters and endorsing the idea that homosexuality is an illness that calls for condolences, Genet was laying claim to his own homosexuality and showing it to be a sin and a crime, a public and private menace designed to intimidate the heterosexual reader. Whereas most other gay novelists concentrated on the young and solitary protagonist, afraid to avow his forbidden desires, or on the gay couple (sensitive, noble, tormented), living in a forest or by the sea or in any event in romantic isolation (the alibi of love), Genet was picturing the gaudy homosexual ghetto of Montmartre, without alibis or medical etiology, and was delineating gay friendships and rivalries and inventing the drag queen for French literature. Indeed, one could say that Genet made a distinction between, on the one hand, the forced sexual relationships that existed between men in the all-male societies of prison, the army, and among those vagabonds too poor to be able to afford women, and, on the other hand, the gay world of Montmartre in which transvestite whores and their pimps mingled, through elective affinities, with artists and criminals in the last flowering of classic bohemianism.

"But why would you want to reduce a great writer like Genet to just *that?*" literary critics, many of them homosexual, complain. (I place to one side another group, those who complain about the very word *gay* or who object to it being applied retrospectively to writers of the past.) In France a closeted gay critic—one of the funniest, most independent, and vitriolic voices in a country known for its excessively genteel journalism (at least in the postwar period)—ridiculed me at the time my biography came out for having abandoned the promise of an early and highly coded, not to say obscure and "poetic" novel such as *Nocturnes for the King of Naples* for the sordid aftermath, my tiresome and overt obsession with homosexuality. Most French critics, I am happy to say, and in the end the publisher as well, were satisfied that I had not turned Genet into a gay folk hero, as they had feared—an absurdity of course, considering how hostile Genet was to everything we would group today under the label "politically correct." Perhaps I surprised or even disappointed some readers by showing that Genet was attracted almost exclusively to heterosexual men. In the seventies he took almost no interest in gay liberation, which he no doubt perceived as a white, middle-class movement, a matter of French domestic politics, at a time when his sole commitment was to the Black Panthers and the Palestinians. To add the final insult, he insisted in one of his last interviews that Freud was the most important friend to homosexuals, since Freud had been the one to put across the theory of universal bisexuality.

But if I was eager to avoid any suggestion that Genet's view of homosexuality was upbeat or communitarian, at the same time I did not want to minimize the key role his sexuality had played in his life and his fiction (if not his theater).

Genet felt that homosexuality had given him an entrée into many different worlds that he would never have known otherwise. He once said that, unlike Proust and Gide, who were liars and cheats, he'd never wanted to downplay his own homosexuality in order to assume a role in the social comedy. "My imagination is plunged into abjection," he said, "but in this respect it is noble, it is pure. I refuse to be an imposter; and if I should happen to go too far when pushing a hero or a plot toward what's horrifying or obscene, at least I'm going in the direction of the truth."[23] In his posthumous masterpiece, *A Prisoner of Love*,[24] he began a whole new meditation on homosexuality and even took up a new theme: the heroism of those who undergo a sex-change operation.

At this point, it might be worth mentioning that, whereas identification with an oppressed minority is seen as limiting ("gay writer"), no limitation is assumed if the individual belongs to a dominant group ("white writer" or "heterosexual painter," for instance).

If I insist on this perfectly obvious truth about the importance of homosexuality to Genet, I do not do so because I'm always on the lookout for the slightest sign of homosexuality. On the contrary, I'm opposed to overly ingenious interpretations of life or art. Typically, the other day I had an argument with an English critic who'd asked me to comment on an essay she'd written about Alberto Giacometti's friendship with Genet. She'd labelled their relationship "homosocial," an interpretation I questioned. I said that Giacometti was not homosexual, though he was an occasional voyeur who liked watching men make love to women. Genet did not fancy Giacometti nor had he ever had sex with another artist or intellectual; neither man, moreover, was the least bit repressed. Both would have eagerly acknowledged a mutual attraction had it existed, but it obviously did not. The word *homosocial* would not apply in any circumstances to two such liberated men, so ready, even eager, to acknowledge their strangest, most unacceptable impulses, unless *homosocial* is used to mean merely an association of two members of the same sex, in which case it designates an uninteresting truism.

If I'm opposed to routine psychological reductionism or any other attempt to formulate a totalizing interpretation of an individual, by the same token I distrust a resistance to the obvious. Genet was a homosexual and wrote about it, just as the adolescent Arthur Rimbaud was homosexual and wrote about it. There may be convincing arguments against speaking of homosexual individuals rather than homosexual acts, although the violent hatred that homosexuality triggers means that anyone whose queerness is known about has had to live, year in and year out, *stigmatized* as a homosexual; this stigma—so constant, so oppressive—does not recognize nice theoretical distinctions between essentialist and social-constructionist explanations of sexual identity.

There may be convincing arguments against projecting contemporary gay cultural categories backward in time and speaking anachronistically about nineteenth-century or even twentieth-century pre-Stonewall "gay life." But what cannot be denied is that homosexuality itself constitutes both a subject and a point of view for many major writers in the twentieth century, and to say that to classify them as homosexual writers is "belittling" means that one considers homosexuality itself to be an unmentionable stain.

I want to be very clear about the fact that I am not defending the idea of a constant and unifying, transhistorical gay sensibility. I'm not even sure what a *sensibility* is; to the degree that it seems to mean anything it means something racist or sexist—what would a *black sensibility* or a *feminine sensibility* be? No, I'm prepared to recognize that there is an experience and not a sensibility, and that even that experience is different for men and for women, for rich and for poor, for whites and for people of color, and that even in a precise category of class, gender, and color that experience varies considerably from decade to decade.

I'm even prepared to entertain the possibility that the homosexuality that Proust or Genet or Hollinghurst spend so much time contemplating and dissecting does not really exist, that it is no more a real, unvarying entity than the Jewishness Kafka analyzes in his letters, or the limits and duties of the feminine role that preoccupy George Eliot in *Middlemarch*. Perhaps homosexuality is a nonsubject: endlessly fertile, ceaselessly shifting, devoid of all stable content, an invitation to musing rather than a fixed object of inquiry. Genet wanted to write an entire book devoted to homosexuality, which he thought would be his highest achievement; that he ended up with only a few painfully self-conscious pages reveals how elusive this nonsubject is if confronted head-on. In fact the most arresting pages are those that are devoted to Egyptian funerary imagery, since Genet linked homosexuality to death, a sterility that could be redeemed only through the fertility of art. That this fascinating cipher, homosexuality, provokes Genet to think about his recurring obsessions—death, sex, and art—reveals that the subject itself is vague only because it is coterminous with the limits of his very being. If homosexuality as a subject lures Gide toward absurd thoughts about monkeys[25] and Proust toward equally preposterous theories about orchids[26] and if all this fantastic botanizing is mixed up with confused thoughts about the Bible and ancient Greece, about the virginity of young girls, and the mating habits of bees, we can only conclude that this nonsubject, homosexuality, is full of exciting conflict and unresolved tensions and can invite its own share of nonsense.

To recapitulate a few of the points I have made up to now, the very category *gay fiction* is accepted or rejected by different cultures according to their varying attitudes toward the ghettoization of culture. In America, the land of lobbies and special interest groups, homosexuals have been styled as the equivalent of an ethnic minority and their literature as its cultural and political expression. In France, a country where a confluence of powerful unified state, intense patriotism, and a vigorous defense of secularism as an ideal creates a taboo against identity politics, the phenomenon of gay literature is treated as a loss of liberty, virtually as a violation of human rights.

Quite distinct from these contradictory national responses to a new category of literature, there is a strategy that closely resembles the French response but is actually a very different maneuver: the bourgeois recuperation of all dissident literatures (and of gay literature in particular) through an appeal to universalism. Middle-class critics may be willing, at least in the English-speaking world, to grant that certain contemporary works of fiction that enjoy a low prestige can be called a part of gay literature, but highly praised works, especially works of the past, are labelled classic and canonical.

To be sure, all serious works of art hope to communicate across racial, national, class, ethnic, generational, or gender barriers, and older homosexual fiction was usually addressed explicitly to a heterosexual reader (most gay art before Stonewall was a form of apologetics). Yet the effort to exempt from the category of gay literature the novels of William Burroughs and Jean Genet, or the poetry of Allen Ginsberg or James Merrill simply because these works are superior, serious, and consecrated, is a rearguard action designed to trivialize the label of gay art. It is also a strategy to recuperate for a purely imaginary, if politically charged, category of "universal art" everything that is admirable, celebrated, or puissant.

But what is this tradition of gay fiction I alluded to earlier? And why is it so loaded with contradictions, fraught with such inner tensions? And why does the very drama of its unfolding generate such hypnotic interest?

I would claim that the characteristic form of gay fiction in the twentieth century, from Proust to Genet to Isherwood, is "autofiction," a convergence of two very different literary traditions, realism and the confession, and that each of these two traditions sets up different expectations on the part of the reader; the troubling synthesis of these two traditions, in fact, is what generates the powerful current of autofiction in general and much of serious gay fiction in particular.

Realism is an eighteenth- and, especially, a nineteenth-century movement in fiction that coincides with the emergence of a prosperous, self-improving, curious, and insecure middle-class readership; the subsequent economic independence of a few writers; a widespread, anxious desire to make sense of the city (which had suddenly grown large and chaotic); and a corresponding appetite for analyzing manners, morals, and passions, no longer held in check or immobilized by traditional social forms. It is primarily a secular form, indicated by the fact that when religion is treated at all it is presented sentimentally and as a program of worldly self-improvement rather than ascetic self-abnegation.

Of course, almost all aesthetic theories are about realism in a larger sense, that is, mimesis, an idea as variable and vast as experience itself. Indeed even the most extreme artistic revolutions often justify themselves by claiming that they have distorted perspective or eliminated punctuation in the interests of a higher realism. Perhaps such innovative movements eschew the notion of documentary realism but typically they invoke the reality of inner experience. Twentieth-century paintings and texts that seem forbiddingly avant-garde and abstract, certainly formalist, almost always rely on the alibi of mimesis, the imitation of human perception or of an objective inanimate reality purged of human conventions. When the American painter Robert Ryman paints all-white canvases, he argues that he is dispensing with illusionary images and revealing the brute reality of the canvas as such, just as when

Alain Robbe-Grillet eliminates all anthropomorphic metaphors he argues that he is rendering with greater clarity the reality of nature.

One of the few exceptions to realism and its constant recourse to nature (human nature or nature *tout court*) is Charles Baudelaire. No one can forget Baudelaire's praise of the "artificial paradise" of hashish and wine, nor his defense of cosmetics, nor his preference of the city over the countryside. As his friend Théophile Gautier wrote of him: "Everything that distanced man and especially woman from the state of nature appeared to him to be a happy invention."[27] Baudelaire saw poetry not as natural but as supernatural, and thought that merely human passions were too violent to suit the aesthetic sentiment, which is a foreglimpse of paradise. Since we are exiled from paradise during our lives, our aesthetic feelings are necessarily melancholic. To be sure other philosophers of aesthetics have seen the supernatural in the sublime, but none has posited nature as the enemy of this vision, though some have suggested that only the artist can interpret nature in such a way as to extract from it its spiritual dimension. Where Baudelaire is radical (of course he was followed by Oscar Wilde and other late nineteenth-century decadents) is in his insistence that nature is antithetical to the beautiful. Not only external nature is the enemy, but even human nature; as Baudelaire writes: "For passion is a *natural* thing, much too natural not to introduce a stinging, discordant note into the domain of pure beauty; too familiar and violent not to scandalize the pure Desires, the gracious Melancholies and the noble Despairs who live in the supernatural region of poetry."[28]

Of course in one particular sense Baudelaire was considered by his contemporaries to be a "realist" since he took an acute interest in low life, in *les bas fonds de Paris*, in the manners and morals of prostitutes, the old, the ill, the poor, the despised. Since at least the eighteenth century the "shocking" has been deemed an aspect of realism. Here realism is contrasted with the religious side of literature and painting—the overwhelmingly dominant tendency of art since its very beginnings. It is no accident that so much of the history of modern art has been associated with scandal—we think of the trials occasioned by the publication of *Les fleurs du mal* and *Madame Bovary,* not to mention the more recent legal judgments concerning James Joyce, D. H. Lawrence, Vladimir Nabokov.

Why is it that these "shocking" writers, these transgressive authors, are also now labeled the most important? Foucault suggests an answer when he writes:

> Texts, books, and discourses really began to have authors (other than mythical, "sacralized" and "sacralizing" figures) to the extent that authors became subject to punishment, that is, to the extent that discourses could be transgressive. In our culture (and doubtless in many others), discourse was not originally a product, a thing, a kind of goods; it was essentially an act—an act placed in the bipolar field of the sacred and the profane, the licit and the illicit, the religious and the blasphemous. Historically, it was a gesture fraught with risks before becoming goods caught up in a circuit of ownership.
>
> Once a system of ownership for texts came into being, once strict rules concerning author's rights, author-publisher relations, rights of reproduction, and related matters were enacted—at the end of the eighteenth and the beginning of the nineteenth century—the possibility of transgression attached to the act of writing took on, more and more, the form of an imperative peculiar to literature. It is as if the author, beginning with the moment at which he was placed in the system of property that characterises our society, compensated for the status that he thus acquired by rediscovering the old bipolar field of discourse, systematically practising transgression and thereby restoring danger to a writing which was now guaranteed the benefits of ownership.[29]

I'm not utterly convinced by Foucault's explanation, though he has certainly pinpointed a phenomenon neglected by everyone before him. I would suggest that prose fiction—enjoying the sacred status of religion inherent in poetry and drama, but motivated by a new documentary urge to record aspects of life previously neglected—awakened contradictory expectations from its public. There is certainly a ceremonial side to literature, to all the arts, symbolized by the French Academy, say, or the Académie des Beaux Arts. There is a minister of culture in most countries, a budget for the arts, the arts define each nationalism, the key works of literature establish the best style in the language, inscriptions on tombs are drawn from literature, and so on.

But there is an equal and opposite tendency toward investigation, muckraking, revelation, toward speaking for the disenfranchised or the silent. In literature this scandalous, politically combative aspect of fiction arises with the bourgeois author, the writer who is no longer dependent on an aristocratic sponsor but who can live from selling his works to a large, anonymous public, a public that is also usually middle class. This is a public that creates, as a parallel to the notion of progress in technology, a corresponding idea of the avant-garde in art—an idea that institutionalizes the transgressive, that sacralizes the scandalous, an idea summed up by the title of the key critical work about abstract expressionism, Harold Rosenberg's *Tradition of the New*.[30]

Just as so much of the "progress" or at least development in painting from the early Renaissance until the invention of photography was in the direction of greater realism—that is, a closer approximation of art and life, whether in the rendering of three-dimensionality, of atmospheric conditions, of human anatomy, of forms and lines (seen near and far, in sunlight or in fog), or of the very act of perception—in the same way "progress" or at least development in literary creation was associated with either an unsparing analysis of the passions

(Benjamin Constant's *Adolphe* [1816]), a depiction of unexciting, middle-class life and its squalid experiments with romance and adultery (Gustave Flaubert's *Madame Bovary* [1857]), or an evocation of immorality (Émile Zola's *Nana* [1880]).

Gay fiction has always been an important tributary to this flood. Proust describes cruising in his chapter on Charlus and Jupien; he also talks about male brothels, sadomasochism, social climbing through homosexuality, a lesbian couple's compulsion to desecrate the sacred memory of an otherwise beloved parent, and the secret signals by which homosexuals recognize each other in *le grand monde*. Here he is as objective, as scientific, as entomological as Honoré Balzac, which is to say, not very scientific at all. Only people who have not read Balzac recently can imagine that his melodramatic plots resemble reality. Balzac set the melodramatic precedent for Proust, especially when he goes over the top in his supposedly accurate descriptions of a kept woman's suicide. In one of his best-known works, *Splendeurs et misères des courtisanes*, we read of the death of Lucien de Rubempré's mistress. Esther knows that Lucien is going to marry another woman for her money. She decides to make a noble gesture, to commit suicide and leave him a small fortune she's acquired; she thinks that if she only had seven or eight millions Lucien would marry her. On the fatal day her friend Val Noble arrives with two pearls. Esther throws one at her greyhound Romeo. "'His name destined him to die thus!' said Esther, and threw the pearl, which Romeo crunched between his teeth. The dog uttered no cry, he spun round and fell in the rigidity of death. This happened while Esther was still speaking her brief elegy."[31] At five that evening Esther dresses up as a bride in a lace dress and a white satin skirt. She receives Lucien for the last time, gives a big party, swallows the other pearl, and dies before learning that she has by coincidence just inherited the seven millions that would have won her happiness with Lucien in marriage. A criminal called Trompela-Mort forges Esther's will to make sure that Lucien receives the money, as the dead woman would have wanted.

In American literature, similarly, realism begins with Hawthorne and Melville, but Hawthorne's stories are so allegorical that they must be treated as mystical fables; and Melville, despite his accurate and detailed descriptions of sailing and whaling, presents actions and dialogue inspired by Shakespeare and the King James version of the Bible, in other words a highly stylized version of reality at odds with the documentary urge found elsewhere in the same books. We could even say, along with the Russian critic Mikhail Bakhtin, that much of the force of these works derives from the "dialogic" encounter between quite different genres of literature, between competing voices and styles.[32]

All I'm trying to suggest is that realism is never simple, that it is always shot through with fantasy and melodrama, but that as a horizon toward which writers march it has long fascinated novelists, perhaps especially gay novelists. Genet, for instance, is anything but a documentary realist, but his descriptions of gay Montmartre or of prison routine are the best records of these phenomena we have from his period. Similarly, John Rechy is a lyric novelist akin to the Beats, but his *City of Night*[33] also remains the best study of the gay underworld of the late fifties in America. Nor is this function of gay fiction by any means exhausted. If I just mention three books at random that I've read recently, you'll see what I mean: Samuel R. Delany's *The Mad Man*,[34] a frightening novel, is the story of a black middle-class American who has sex with homeless men, white and black. It is so compelling partly because it makes voyeurs out of its readers; if we felt it was wholly invented from the imagination we would read it with much less horrified interest. Similarly, *Crystal Boys* by Pai Hsien-Yung,[35] although confused and amateurish as a novel, intrigues us because it gives us a glimpse into contemporary gay life in Taiwan among rent boys and other outcasts. Finally,

René de Ceccaty's recent nonfiction book on the lesbian novelist Violette Leduc[36] freely mixes his own long obsession with her work with parallel scenes from his own intimate life—a startlingly new way to write personal criticism that enjoys all the queasy-making and exhilarating freedom of gay autofiction.

If gay autofiction does seem slippery and free it does so, I would argue, because it not only embodies the continuing documentary ambitions of the realistic novel, but because it also participates just as actively in a very different tradition, the confession, which is by its very nature religious and exemplary. Most ancient art, whether it is Greek sculpture or Egyptian tomb paintings or the poems from the Greek anthology or African sculpture, had a religious dimension, a social, celebratory aspect, sometimes a funerary function. We must not forget that even the Greek comedies and tragedies were propitiations of the gods. In a Christian context the religious function of art continued in every domain until the eighteenth century.

I think it was the nineteenth century English art critic Arthur Symons who called art "spilt religion." Certainly the *philosophy* of art was dominated by spiritual if not strictly religious thought in the eighteenth and nineteenth centuries down to our own days.

Today what has happened is that the two traditions of realism and spirituality have come together, and they exert strangely unequal and contradictory pressures on the artist or on the consumer of art.

One of the key figures in the nineteenth and twentieth centuries is the artist-martyr. Perhaps the prototype is Van Gogh, the inspired genius tormented by madness who manages to sell just one painting during his lifetime.[37] Or we are drawn to the life of Antonin Artaud, the madman whose body was wracked by electroshock administered by hostile psychiatrists, whose final work is nothing but a scream, whose grandiose and influential ideas about the theater of cruelty foundered into madness. Or we prefer to read about the life of Fernando Pessoa (his nonlife) than to read his poetry.

Today the artist is a saint who writes his own life. The fusion of autobiography and fiction has been a slow process, still not entirely achieved. Writers have always drawn on their own experience, of course, but usually in highly disguised forms, or they have written straightforward confessions, although any sustained look at Rousseau's *Confessions* or Benjamin Constant's *Journaux Intimes* will show how devious or partial even such so-called "full disclosures" can be.

We should not forget that the first autobiography in English was the confessions of Margery Kempe, a would-be saint of the fourteenth century[38] (and, perhaps not coincidentally *Margery Kempe* is the title and subject of an extraordinary new gay novel by Robert Glück).[39] Going even farther back, we could mention Saint Augustine's *Confessions*.

The autobiographical urge, from its very beginnings, has been the site where two codes—the realistic and the spiritual—have crossed. If Arthur Schopenhauer, for instance, placed biography and autobiography above history (if still below poetry), he did so because he felt biography—and especially autobiography—"in a narrow sphere shows us the conduct of men in all its nuances and forms, the excellence, the virtue, and even the holiness of individuals, the perversity, meanness and malice of most, the profligacy of the many."[40] In other words, whereas history shows us formal long-shot panoramas of crowds—especially armies—autobiography gives us the individual, in all his glowing detail, remarkably free of lies, as Schopenhauer believes, since he contends that writing a confession calls for honesty. The traditional lives of the saints were highly formulaic: the mortifications, the early calling, the doubting friends and family members, finally the decisive, convincing miracles, and the edifying death.

Now the autobiographical novel enjoys the prestige of confession and the freedom of fiction, yet within that rather vague context there is room for lots of new, concrete, idio-syncratic detail, as long as it does not depart too far from the ideal of the martyr. Genet can question the very roots of our way of perceiving the self, as long as that self is the suffering outcast child who is tortured by society in prison, yet emerges triumphant through his art. Whereas Proust recasts his own sexuality, conceals his Jewish origins, and ascribes a social importance to himself that apparently he did not enjoy, he nevertheless does not fail to portray himself as a martyr to love and to art. For him love is always unreciprocated and his book is a long dissection of hopeless passion, just as the book itself is a testament to his own martyrdom to art.

By now you're probably annoyed with all my second thoughts, perhaps the very abundance of my theory-spinning, but I can't resist adding here that I am rather dubious about my entire enterprise today. When one attempts to relate the history of art to the history of society, has one really said any-thing? Paul Veyne, the great historian, has given us this warn-ing in *Les Grecs ont-ils cru à leurs mythes?* He asserts that to relate literary history

> to society is an undertaking that noone has accomplished and which is perhaps less false than empty. The historicity of literary history is not there. It resides in the enormous unconscious changes that over three centuries have affected what we have not ceased to designate with the illusory words "literature," "the beautiful," "taste," and "art." Not only have relationships between literature and society changed; the Beautiful itself, Art itself have been transformed. Indeed, the core of these realities contains nothing immutable to leave to the philosophers. They are historical and not philosophical. There is no core.[41]

Undoubtedly the words I have used—realism, spirituality, mimesis—are misleading words and mean something different in each epoch, but if my proposals have no historic validity perhaps they at least blaze an imaginary tradition that imaginative artists at least imagine they are following.

If I put aside these scruples for a moment (which I'm not at all certain I'm permitted to do), I might conclude by asking why should homosexual writers be especially drawn to autofiction and its double heritage?

The form itself, which is neither purely fact nor fiction, gives the writer both the prestige of confession (this is my story, only I have the right to tell it, and no one can challenge my authority in this domain) *and* the total freedom of imaginative invention (I'm a novelist, I can say whatever I please, and you can't hold me responsible for the opinions expressed by my characters, nor even by my narrator).

This wavering between authority and unaccountability, this way of saying both "This really happened and I alone have survived to tell the story" *and* "How dare you assume I'm speaking of my own life?"—this doubleness reflects perhaps the unfinished business and ambiguous status of homosexual identity itself. Is that identity an eternal essence, biologically or theologically determined and unvarying, a quiddity that the individual very slowly uncovers within himself? This possibility corresponds to the confessional face of autofiction. Or is homosexuality created by society? Does its very formation mark a stage in the public invasion of the private sphere, in the social colonization of individual consciousness? If so, the novel remains the most fluent way of showing in a dramatic context the dynamic tension between society and the individual. Or yet again is the particular form homosexuality takes in any given era the result of a social elaboration of a biological predisposition? Wouldn't such a formula correspond well to both the creative and the documentary claims of this peculiarly modern literary form?

At this point, in summing up, it would be rhetorically tempting to come out in favor of another possibility, a humanist reaffirmation of the power of the individual to *shape* his or her identity, to overcome adversity, to impose his or her will on circumstances.

I will not fall prey to this temptation, but I would suggest that the gay novel, in adumbrating the arbitrariness of social conventions, by challenging the "naturalness" of gender roles, by proving how the deviant, sometimes desperate outsider can occasionally realize his desires despite all the force of societal condemnation—that this fictional reconstruction of a historic struggle is one of the most gripping examples we have of dissident literature as well as the one most suited to the genius of autofiction as a genre.

For in the contemporary gay novel, as I've tried to show, the alternation between the sacred tradition of exposing an exemplary life (exemplary in its excesses, its courage, its martyrdom) and the secular tradition of documenting a particular life in sensuous fullness and detail, in its social context and in all its idiosyncratic individuality—this alternation best dramatizes the double heritage of gay writing as an *apologia pro vita sua* and as a sexologist's case history.

THE OPPRESSOR
AND THE OPPRESSED

Taslima Nasreen

I

I was born free. I was born in a sovereign independent country, namely Pakistan. My birth place was the Eastern part of that country, which was separated from the other part by a thousand miles. When I was nine years old, our part of Pakistan threw out the oppressive ruler of West Pakistan, and Bangladesh was born. Naturally I too was born twice: first as a citizen of Pakistan, then as a citizen of Bangladesh. My father had to change his nationality three times. He was born in an undivided India. When the Western rulers left the Indian subcontinent, dividing it into two separate parts, he became a citizen of Pakistan. And after the birth of Bangladesh, he became a citizen of this newborn country.

Though I have no personal memories of British rule in the Indian subcontinent, I feel I am a child of the colonial era, because centuries of British rule had a direct bearing not only on the partition of a great country but also inevitably on the emergence of Bangladesh. As a parting kick, the foreign imperialist power divided the country on religious lines in the name of the rights of the minorities. It invented the idea of physical partition and unfortunately both the nationalist and the religious leaders of the time endorsed it. That the idea was ridiculous was self-evident. Millions of Muslims remained in India after the partition despite their having been granted a homeland, itself divided into two different parts. And not only was it absurd, but millions had to go through intense suffering for this senseless arrangement. Millions of both Hindus and Muslims were uprooted from their homes and had to migrate to another part of the country. In fact, even after four decades, the curse of this decision retains its power.

I am no historian or political analyst. When I look around me, I feel it was the British imperialists who were primarily responsible for partition and that it was a failure on the part of the leaders of the subcontinent that they were unable to detect this evil design. They succumbed to it and brought doom on themselves. The birth of Bangladesh has demonstrated the absurdity of the partition of the country on the basis of religion. The common factor between the two parts of Pakistan was that the majority of the people were Muslims. Otherwise their language, culture, dress, and way of life were completely different. Like other colonial powers in the past, the rulers of the western part wanted to impose their culture and language on the Muslims of the eastern part; hence the revolt. Of course, there was economic exploitation also. But in the development of Bengali nationalism in East Pakistan, language and culture played a pivotal role. Islam could not keep its children together. Though they professed the same faith, the oppressed threw out the oppressor. So, without any experience of a direct encounter with imperialism, I feel that I understand it, its nature and its purposes, and at the same time I understand colonialism too.

Looking at the recent history of Bangladesh, I can guess how British paramountcy in India was established and how it could keep so large a nation in subjection for so long. The Mughal Empire was on its last legs in the nineteenth century. India was in the doldrums. Intrigue followed intrigue. It was not difficult to find power-crazy collaborators. The East India Company made the best of collaborators. In Bengal, everybody knows about the Battle of Plassey (1757). Bankim Chandra, one of the greatest intellectuals of nineteenth-century Bengal, described the so-called war as "fun-play."[1] To quote a modern historian:

> Plassey . . . was a transaction, not a battle, a transaction by which the compradors of Bengal, led by Jagat Seth, sold the Nawab Mir Qasim to the East India Company. The Nawab's Generals, already in league with the Hindu merchant princes and their British allies, did not fight, and the treacherous General, Mir Jafar, received as a price of his betrayal, the Nawabi of Bengal.[2]

The East India Company had gained a foothold and after the defeat of Mir Qasim at Buxar in 1764, they obtained *Diwani*, that is, the right to administrate the revenues of the rich territories of Bengal, Bihar, and Orissa. After that, nobody could stop the British. Other European competitors had to bow out. Local resistance was also crushed. Gradually the trading company became the master of a vast country inhabited by millions of people.

Similarly, in the struggle for the emergent Bangladesh, we found collaborators at work in the name of religion. They joined the exploiters of West Pakistan and played in various ways into their hands. They even killed hundreds and thousands of Bengali patriots, intellectuals, and politicians. The rulers of West Pakistan followed the British example in another way. They tried to divide the people and rule forever in Bangladesh, the erstwhile East Pakistan, which is inhabited not only by Muslims but also by a sizeable number of Hindus and some Buddhists and Christians. The culture of Bangladesh, like Indian culture, is mixed. Nevertheless, West Pakistan and its allies tried not only to drive a wedge between Hindus and Muslims, but even to purify the Bengali language in Islamic fashion. This trick, I assume, they learned from their earlier masters, the British.

Imperialism, as I understand it, is not just forcible physical occupation of a land. A people can be subjugated properly only if it can be intellectually subjugated first. This can be done by imposing the "superior" culture of the rulers on the culture of the ruled, which is labelled as inferior. This was also done in the case of India. The orientalists worked hard and sincerely to unveil India's past. Both ancient and medieval India were brought to light through their efforts. But they could not stop an imperialist spokesman like Thomas Macaulay from stating about the British orientalists that he had "never found one among them who could deny that a single shelf of a good European library was worth the whole native literature of India and Arabia."[3] The great debate in the fourth decade of the nineteenth century between orientalists and anglicists ended with the latter undisputed victors.

Of course, there were enlightened Indians like Rammohun Roy who thought modern European philosophy and science were important for Indian youth. In a letter to Lord Amherst in 1823, Rammohun pointed out at length how Indian students could waste valuable time by studying Sanskrit dramas, the speculative philosophy of Vedanta, obsolete interpretations of Vedic passages in *Mimangsa*, and the subtleties of the *Naya Sastras* if they clung to oriental education. He wrote:

> if it had been intended to keep the British nation in ignorance of real knowledge, the Baconian philosophy would not have been allowed to displace the system of the schoolmen, which was the best calculated to perpetuate ignorance. . . . But as the improvement of the native population is the object of the Government, it will consequently promote a more liberal and enlightened system of education, embracing Mathematics, Natural Philosophy, Chemistry, Anatomy, with other useful sciences.[4]

In the same year, Rammohun launched a protest campaign against the Press Ordinance of 1823 and wrote to the King in Council thus: "where no freedom of the Press existed, and grievances consequently remained unrepresented and unredressed, innumerable revolutions have taken place in all parts of the globe, or, prevented by the armed forces of the Government, the people continued ready for insurrection."[5] Thus the spirit of modern education and the spirit of freedom of expression converged in Rammohun Roy as early as 1823.

Rammohun had supporters in Bengal too. Naturally English education started to gain ground. The Hindu College was established in 1817, and by 1857 three universities were founded in India, where education meant mostly Western education in which the medium of instruction was English.

Though Macaulay wanted to make Indians subservient to British rule by imparting English education and creating an anglicized community, he also realized that "having become instructed in European languages they [the Indians] may, in some future age, demand European institutions."[6] This showed foresight. Another civilian, Mountstuart Elphinstone, commented that to educate the native was a duty, but it was "our highroad back to Europe."[7] Trevelyan, on the other hand, while testifying before the Select Committee of the House of Commons in 1853, said "familiarly acquainted with us by means of our literature, the Indian youth almost cease to regard us as foreigners.... As long as the natives are left to brood over their former independence, their sole specific for improving their condition is the immediate and total expulsion of the English."[8]

Actually, the idea was picked up by the Indians too at an early stage. The students of Hindu College had a young teacher named Henry Louis Vivian Derozio. He was a man of letters and a radical. One of his students wrote: "He used to impress upon them the sacred duty of thinking for themselves—to be in no way influenced by idols mentioned by Bacon—to live and die for truth—to cultivate all the virtues, shunning vice in every shape. He often read examples from ancient history of the love of justice, patriotism, philanthropy and self-abnegation."[9] A contemporary newspaper reported that in Calcutta, one bookseller advertised Tom Paine's *Age of Reason* at one rupee per copy. He imported one hundred copies and immediately sold out.[10] Derozio's young disciples were willing to pay five rupees for a copy of the book.[11] Voltaire, Locke, Bacon, and Hume were widely read and discussed among them. A contemporary English journal wrote: "in the matter of politics they are all radicals, and are followers of Benthamite principles. The very word Tory is a sort of ignominy among them."[12] Under the inspiration of Derozio, the Hindu College students founded many academic associations and brought out several periodicals. They discussed "free will, free ordination, fate, faith, the sacredness of truth, the high duty of cultivating virtue, the meanness of vice, the nobility of patriotism,"[13] and so on. The object of one such society was to acquire and disseminate useful knowledge about the condition of the country. In this society, when a member was reading a paper on the "East India Company's Criminal Judicature and Police under the Bengal Presidency," the principal of the Hindu College interrupted the reader by observing that the paper contained treasonable matters. The president of the Society reminded the principal: "You are only a visitor on this occasion and possess no right to interrupt a member of this society in the utterance of his opinions."[14] "This is a remarkable instance of the sturdy spirit of independence by which the students of Hindu College were inspired."[15] On another occasion, on December 25, 1830, the Derozians hoisted the *tricouleur* of the French Revolution over the Ochterloney Monument in Calcutta.[16]

A natural and logical consequence of these actions and movements, which emerged essentially from English contacts and education, was the birth and growth of nationalism. This eventually engulfed India and took on dimensions such that the British rulers had to withdraw from the subcontinent. Where rationalism had been the watchword of the first generation of English-educated Bengalis, that of the second generation was nationalism. From the seed of freedom of thought and expression sprouted the struggle for the freedom of the country and the nation. It is interesting to note that English rule bred its own destruction and that the struggle for freedom from English rule was inspired and carried out by the English-educated people of the subcontinent. Of course, Gandhiji's mass movement became widespread not only in the cities and towns but in the fields and factories. But the leadership, by and large, was drawn from the English-educated middle and upper-middle classes. In fact many of the national leaders were educated in England. True, most English-educated people remained loyal to the Raj and served the foreign master in various capacities, as Macaulay and his supporters had expected. But many of them, even among the would-be bureaucrats, thought it ignominious to work for English rulers. The ICS, the Indian Civil Service, described by some as the "Heaven Born Service," was for many years reserved for aspirants from the English middle class. Though competitive exams were introduced by the middle of the nineteenth century, we hear that by 1915 there were still only sixty-three ICS Indians; only 5 percent of the service was Indian.[17] Later the number was raised, but the "steel framework of the Raj" effectively remained until the end a preserve of the British. Naturally, for any Indian to be recruited as a member of the ICS was considered a remarkable achievement. Yet there were dropouts too. I can think of at least two names who instead of serving the alien rulers became freedom fighters. Today they are remembered in the subcontinent as immortal fighters. One is Aurobindo Ghose and the other Netaji Subhas Chandra Bose. Both were Bengalis. Ghose spread the cult of the bomb at the turn of the century[18] and Bose raised an army to fight the British during World War II.[19]

The struggle for freedom in India had many facets. Gandhiji believed in nonviolent mass movement. So did most of his disciples. There were moderates and extremists in the National Congress. Outside the Congress fold, there were other political parties whose creeds were different from each other and who continued their struggles through various methods. If we put aside the religious fundamentalists, by and large, India's struggle for freedom, whether led by the liberals or the extremists, drew its inspiration from sources outside India. Here is the relevance of British imperialism and

British education. Even Gandhiji talked not only of the Gita but also of John Ruskin, Henry David Thoreau, and Leo Tolstoy. Bengali revolutionaries spoke of Giuseppe Mazzini, Giuseppe Garibaldi, and the Sinn Fein movement in Ireland.

II

Yes, there are words and words and words. Words may express servitude, words may also shout defiance. There are words that mean compliance and there are words of protest too. Some words are for conformity, some express resentment. Some words are uttered by the weak and the obedient, some by the self-respecting and rebellious soul. Yes, even among women words varying in meaning are in use. I will focus on the language of the dissident women whom I have come across in my own culture. Before that a few words on the emergence of this rebellious tribe in Bengal.

British rule and English education had its impact on the lives of the women of the Indian subcontinent also. *Suttee*, or the burning of the widow with the dead husband, was prohibited, and polygamy and child marriage among the Hindus were abolished. Civil marriage and the remarriage of widows were introduced, and the need was felt for girl children to be educated. Each of these reforms was important for the women of the subcontinent—especially for the majority Hindu community. For them, an era of enlightenment was ushered in by the joint effort of the educated urban middle class and the British rulers. Though schools and colleges for girls were not numerous, and though the scope of their education remained very limited, the little learning that parents or husbands bestowed on girls to make them better wives had its "undesirable" effect on young women too. It is said of the Bengali girl that even though her heart rends, her lips never part to speak (*book phhaathe to mookhh phhothe naa*). Well, they have started to speak out now!

Previously, Bengali women had a different sort of language. Dr. Sukumar Sen, a distinguished Bengali linguist, noted in a discussion of their language:

> (a) women's speech is, generally speaking, more conservative than that of men. . . . Women's speech retains archaic features when these have long disappeared from the dialect of men. (b) Women's vocabulary contains a very large number of intensive words and emphatic particles as well as pejorative expletives. . . . (c) Euphemism is one of the great characteristics of women's speech. Women are naturally shy of mentioning some parts of the human anatomy and some functions of human physiology. (d) Women are generally superstitious. . . . Women of some peoples are forbidden to mention the name of their husbands or their superiors. (e) Women's vocabulary is much more limited than that of man. . . . (f) Women are exceedingly fond of pejorative terms and expressions. They are masters in the exchange of smart taunts and saucy ridicules.[20]

Dr. Sen informs us that though there are exceptions in Sanskrit literature, women and lower-class people generally talk *Prakrit* (the vulgar language) while men have the privilege of talking *Sanskrit*, the chaste, adorned language. Obviously, this indicates the inferior position of women in society.[21] Naturally, there many derogatory words used to denote women in Bengali. But lo and behold, women also had some words at their disposal to bestow upon men who proved not beyond criticism. In medieval Bengali poetry we occasionally find married women who are outspoken in criticizing their husbands in vulgar terms and even refer to the sexual impotence of their aged husbands (*Naariganer Pat inindaa*). Many Bengali proverbs are also quite derogatory about men. In proverbs, we find women critical of their tormentors, not least of their husbands. I would mention just a few of these: *eto kore kori ghor, tobuminse base par,* "I take such pains with running the household, still my man treats me distantly"; *kaaje knoodre khete dedre bachane maare poodriye poodriye,* "he is idle at work but eats for two, while he burns me alive with his complaints"; *darbaare mookhh maa peye ghare ese maar thhhengaay,* "not finding an opportunity to speak at the court, he comes home and beats his wife"; *bhhat deoaar kshamataa naai kil maaraar gosaain,* "he has no capacity for giving me food, but is game for dealing fisticuffs"; *yjaar janya karlaam yjo sei bale paithane sho,* "he whom I serve so faithfully asks me to lie at his footstool"; *bhhat deoy naa bhhat aare, bhhaat deoy gat are,* "my husband does not give me food, my body earns it," and so on.[22]

With the spread of education, many a change could be observed among urban middle-class women. They took up the pen to express themselves. Later, they also became political activists. Between 1905 and 1939, a number of Bengali women joined secret societies for winning freedom by violent means. Some even took up arms. Here I would like to discuss what happened after they started pouring out their hearts on paper. Malavika Karlekar notes:

Almost 400 works by Bengali women were estimated to have been written between 1856 and 1910. These ranged from short poems to full-length novels and autobiographies. During the same period, to cater to a growing readership, twenty one periodicals which dealt primarily with women's issues were being published. Interestingly, women were associated in various editorial capacities with these publications. More specifically, over the last century, there is a record of at least fifty autobiographies and autobiographical sketches having been written by Bengali women.[23]

They wrote about their sufferings. They wrote about the agonies they experienced. Most of them remained conformist. But some did not confine themselves to contesting the lives that patriarchal society had charted out for them; they also raised questions. Some demanded equal status. Some even thought about economic freedom. In a society where religious and traditional rules prevailed, some women even in those days did not hesitate to express their doubts. I will give a few instances. One Kailashvasini Devi, whose English-educated husband became Westernized, wrote: "I don't believe in Hindu rituals, but nonetheless I observe them. The reason for this is that, if I slacken even a bit, my husband will cease being a Hindu. . . . Those who have brains do not observe the Hindu religion. I do not believe in Hindu religion. But I will never tell my husband this."[24] Another Bengali woman, after visiting many holy places, concludes: "at that time there was an element of childishness. I still believe that going on Tirthhas [pilgrimages] is a good thing. But now I view them with a certain degree of affection—in the same way that I love my children and those who are my own. But by doing all these I do not believe that I will achieve salvation."[25]

Nearer home, I would like to quote a rebellious Muslim woman, Begum Rokeya Sakhawat Hossein. She was against *purdah*. She was in favor of educating Muslim girls. She knew that religion was at the root of the subjection of women. She wrote:

In the history of mankind, when someone became known to many for his talent or genius, he would claim that he was a God or a man sent to earth by God. . . . I do not know whether religious scriptures were handed to man by God. Nobody is sure of that. I feel if any messenger of God had been sent to rule women he would not have confined his activity to Asia. Why did the messenger of God not go to Europe? From America to the poles, everywhere women would be ruled by man. Why was it not so decreed? Is this God Asia's God only?[26]

When Indians educated in the English language became restless and felt a strong urge to make the country free, Bengali women, for whom the doors of modern education had just opened, also made a silent revolution by crossing the boundary of the domain marked out for them by patriarchal society. They stepped into the male's realm. If men can discard age-old traditions and religious rituals, why can't we? If men can organize societies, run periodicals, write books, why can't we? Women gradually absorbed the male language of protest. Early autobiographies by women are "characterised by an earthy dialect and evocative phrases, women's use of language, like that of the *Chotolok* (common folk), was rich in myth, ritual, fantasy and folk songs."[27] William Carey in his *Kathopokathan* (Book of Conversations) in 1801 recorded three different dialects of Bengali women in three different situations—in Bazaars, in Anthapurs (*zenana* or women's wing of the house), and when they quarreled. Later writings of Bengali women show that they became familiar with the outer world and absorbed much of the refined male language in their writings. At that point, they were able to question patriarchs in their own terms and in the same language. I think this is an attainment of which women should be proud. If some people long for the lost feminine voice in the writings of modern Bengali women, they are asking for the lost world where women's language was the language of the subordinate and meek, the subservient. I do not believe in a gender divide in language. Sexual equality should be the norm here too.

With the emergence of the middle class and the spread of higher education, Bengali girls gained the chance to be educated in various disciplines. As a result, even in Bangladesh we find women engaged in different professions, though they may be few in number. There are doctors, lawyers, school and college teachers, government officers, and executives in business organizations. These days, Bengali women are active in the creative fields too. There are women poets, novelists, essayists, journalists, movie stars, theater artists, musicians, and painters.

Some women writers are fairly popular, but they write the kind of novels or poems that are expected of them. This is the expectation of men, which, because of the dominance of patriarchy, is shared by most female readers. Society as a whole expects polite, soft, docile, and submissive women, so the readers of women writers expect from them a soft, decent, and conformist story. Women poets "should" also write love poems that are lyrical and betray femininity as patriarchy defines it. One is surprised to see how women writers describe feminine beauty in their writings. Their proto-types are simply borrowed from male writers. It seems that these women writers have forgotten even to look at their own images in the mirror. I have not come across the description of a hero's physical beauty in any woman writer of my country. Though the heroine is longing to meet him, she is shy of the physical attributes of her adored hero. But as I have said, I do not believe in the requirement that femininity should ooze from whatever a woman author writes. I have deliberately broken the gender barrier in my writing and used words that male writers would like to think belong entirely to them. My vocabulary does not necessarily remain content with the so-called feminine words.

One of the charges against my writing is that I write pornography. This is absolute nonsense. Throughout the ages, it is men who have produced pornography. What I have done is simply describe women's desires and the suffering inflicted on them by sexual abuse. In fact, I feel aspects of female sexuality are totally ignored or fantasized about by most of the male writers in my country. What I do might be labelled a corrective measure. As every woman has a mind and body of her own, they must have a language of the mind and body too. Why should I be described as a pornographer when I honestly try to create and record this language in my writings? Male critics are simply shocked because here, perhaps for the first time, they have met a woman writer who dared to step into the male domain and one not at all ashamed to talk about a subject that is considered totally forbidden for women.

Again, I dare to write against male-made religion. I believe that women are oppressed by every religion. If any religion allows the persecution of people of different faiths, if any religion keeps people in ignorance, if any religion keeps women in slavery, then I cannot accept that religion. Freedom for women will never be possible until they cross the barrier of religion and patriarchy.

What I have written thus far relates mainly to urban middle-class Hindu women. The situation during the freedom struggle was different for Muslim women. Even after independence and the emergence of Bangladesh as a sovereign country, the difference between the plight of Hindu women and Muslim women remains. But with the emergence of a Muslim middle class and the spread of women's education in the community, signs of change are gradually beginning to appear. The pattern is more or less the same as that experienced by middle-class Muslim women from the middle of the nineteenth century to the early decades of this century. But the pace of progress is slower in our society for the simple reason that, compared to Hinduism, Islam is rather orthodox and not amenable to change. Raising questions or discussing subjects that are considered taboo for women may lead one into great trouble. I myself am perhaps a case in point. Compared to my feminist sisters in the West, I have written little about patriarchy, religion, man-woman relations, and the rights of women. Nevertheless, I have been marked out as an enemy of Islam and of my own society. I do not mind being persecuted and hunted by mullahs and their frenzied followers. I am happy that I have penetrated a bastion of patriarchy guarded by frantic religious orthodoxies. As a free human being, I have entered this courtyard not with a sword in my hand, but with a simple instrument: the pen. I do not write in vulgar terms; I use the refined vocabulary of men and throw questions into their faces as a free human being. To conclude, I should like to quote from one of my poems:

> *You're a girl*
> *and you'd better not forget*
> *that when you step over the threshold of your house*
> *men will look askance at you.*
> *When you walk down the lane*
> *men will follow you and whistle.*
> *When you cross the lane and step into the main road*
> *men will revile you and call you a loose woman.*
> *If you are weak*
> *you'll turn back,*
> *and if you're not*
> *you'll keep going*
> *as you're going now.*[28]

ON CHAOS

Gore Vidal

Last November 4, three days before the election that produced a congressional majority for the duller half of the American single-party system, I addressed the National Press Club in Washington. I do this at least once a year not because writer-journalists are present, wise and fearless as they are, but because cable television carries one's speech without editing or editorializing. This useful service, known as C-Span, specializes in covering such eccentricities as myself and the British House of Commons.

I reflected upon the confusion that each of us is feeling as this unlamented century and failed millennium draw, simultaneously, to a close, and there is no hint of order in the world—and is *that* such a bad thing? As for my own country, I said that there is now a whiff of Weimar in the air. Three days later, to no one's surprise, only a third of the electorate bothered to vote. The two-thirds that abstained now realize that there is no longer a government which even pretends to represent them. The great—often international and so unaccountable—cartels that finance our peculiar political system are the only entities represented at Washington. Therefore, in lieu of representative government, we have call-in radio programs, where the unrepresented can feel that, for a minute or two, their voices are heard, if not heeded. In any case, a system like ours cannot last much longer and, quite plainly, *something is about to happen.* I should note that one Rush Limbaugh, a powerful radio demagogue, greeted November's Republican landslide as a final victory over what he called the age of Lenin and Gore Vidal. It was not clear whether he meant Moscow's Lenin or Liverpool's Lennon. Then, to my amazement the *Wall Street Journal,* where I lack admirers, took seriously my warning and "*What* is going to happen?" is a question now being asked among that 2 or 3 percent of the population who are interested in politics or indeed in anything other than personal survival in a deteriorating society.

Certainly, I have no idea what is going to happen, but as the ineffable Ross Perot likes to say, it won't be pretty.

I have now lived through more than two-thirds of the twentieth century, as well as through at least one-third of the life of the American Republic. I can't say that I am any wiser now than I was when I first began to look about me at the way things are, or rather at the way that things are made to look to be, but I am beginning to detect an odd sort of progression in world affairs. And I have noticed lately that I am not alone.

Recently, the literary critic, Harold Bloom, in the somewhat quixotic course of establishing a Western literary canon, divided human history into phases that cyclically repeat.[1] First, there is a theocratic age, next an aristocratic age, followed by a democratic age, which degenerates into chaos and out of which some new idea of divinity will emerge to unite us all in a brand-new theocratic age, and the cycle begins again. Bloom rather dreads the coming theocratic age but as he—and I—will never see it, we can settle comfortably into the current chaos where the meaning of meaning is an endlessly cozy subject, and Heisenberg's principle is undisputed law of the land, at least from where each of us is situated.

I shall not discuss Bloom's literary canon, which, like literature itself, is rapidly responding if not to chaos to entropy. But I do have some thoughts on the cyclic nature of the way human society evolves as originally posited by Plato in the eighth book of the *Republic* and further developed by Giovanni Batista Vico in his *Scienza Nuova*.

Professor Bloom skips Plato and goes straight to Vico, an early eighteenth-century Neapolitan scholar who became interested in the origins of Roman law. The deeper Vico got into the subject, the further back in time he was obliged to go, specifically to Greece. Then he got interested in how it was that the human race was able to create an image of itself for itself. At the beginning there appears to have been an animistic belief in the magic of places and in the personification of the elements as gods. To Vico, these legends, rooted in prehistory, were *innate* wisdom. Plainly, he was something of a Jungian before that cloudy Swiss fact. But then the age of the gods was challenged by the rise of individual men. Suddenly, kings and heroes are on the scene. They in turn give birth to oligarchies, to an aristocratic society where patricians battle for the first place in the state. In time, the always exciting game of who will be king of the castle creates a tyranny that will inspire the people at large to rebel against the tyrants and establish republics that, thanks to man's nature, tend to imperial acquisitiveness and so, in due course, these empire-republics meet *their* natural terminus in, let us say, the jungles of Vietnam.

What happens next? Vico calls the next stage Chaos, to be followed by a new Theocratic Age. This process is, of course, pure Hinduism, which was never to stop leaking into Greek thought from Pythagoras to the neo-Platonists and even now into the alert mind of my friend Allen Ginsberg and of numerous California surfers and ceramists. Birth, death, chaos, then rebirth, and so—on and on and on.

But though Vico's mind was brilliant and intuitive, the history that he had to deal with necessarily left out science—as we know it and he did not—and we must now ponder how chaos may yet organize itself with the use of computers and faxes and the means to control all the people all the time, including taping the private conversations of the British royal family from, let us say, a command post at Cheltenham. Chaos—our current condition—may prove to be altogether too interesting to make order of. Will the next god be a computer? In which case, a *tyrant* god for those of us who dwell in computer-challenged darkness.

A characteristic of our present chaos is the dramatic migration of tribes. They are on the move from east to west, from south to north. Liberal tradition requires that borders must always be open for those in search of safety or even the pursuit of happiness. In the case of the United States, the acquisition of new citizens from all the tribes of earth has always been thought to be a very good thing. But now with so many billions of people on the move, even our great republic is looking less and less like a country and more and more like the international lounge of some third-world airport. In short, the human chaos is now poignantly noticeable.

So, what is going to happen? Well, Norway is large enough and empty enough to take in forty or fifty million homeless Bengalis. If the Norwegians say that, all in all, they would rather *not* take them in, is this to be considered racism? I think not. It is simply self-preservation, the first law of species. So even those of us usually to be found on the liberal end of the political spectrum are quite aware that the tribes must stay put and be helped to improve wherever it is that they were placed by nature or by our dissolving empires, to which all sorts of odd chickens are now coming home to roost.

I have noticed that whenever race is mentioned in much of the United States or Germany, there is often a spasm of hysteria. "Race is a myth!" a young German told me after a speech I had made. I agreed with him that the *stereotypes* of race tend to be mythical, not to mention mischievous, but that, as world climate changes and populations increase, the tribes are on the move, and the racial composition of Europe, say, has changed more in the last fifty years than in the previous five hundred. As an American, I think that this is not such a bad thing, but there does come a moment when there are simply too many people on the move and not enough space or resources to accommodate them in the old established societies. I asked the young German if I might use the word "tribe" instead of race. No, no, the word tribe is even politically more incorrect than race. How then, I asked, are we to describe your skinheads in Dresden who are beating up

Turkish workers? Or Bosnian Muslims being killed by Bosnian Serbs. "Multiculturalism," was the stern answer. But, I said, American blacks and whites are often at each other's throats and one of the reasons they are is that they are not only *not* multicultural but they share the same American culture, in which hatred of the other plays so vigorous a part. I concluded my message to the Germans by saying that the white race is only 16 percent of the world's population with many well-deserved enemies. I suggested that the United States, Canada, Russia, and Western Europe form a northern alliance in order to survive economically in an Asian world. I was promptly denounced by a Swiss German for invoking the yellow peril. More chaos.

It is a sign of true chaos that any realism about, let us say, world trade and the challenge of cheap labor to expensive labor can easily be derailed by invoking race, religion, and the nation state.

As we start the second millennium of what we in our Western section of the globe are amused to call the Christian era, we should be aware, of course, that most of the world's tribes are, happily for them, not Christian at all. Also, most of us who are classified as Christians and live in nations where this form of monotheism was once all powerful now live in a secular world. So chaos does have its pleasures. But then as Christian presuppositions do not mean anything to others (recently Buddhists sternly reminded the pope of this in Sri Lanka), so, too, finally, Plato and his perennially interesting worldview don't make much sense when applied to societies such as ours. I like his conceit of the political progression of societies and a case can be made for it, as Vico did. But Plato, as political thinker, must be taken with Attic salt, which John Jay Chapman brilliantly supplies in an essay recently discovered in his archives.

I doubt if many of you will even know Chapman's name. He died in 1933. He was America's greatest essayist after

Emerson. He is almost as little known in his native land as elsewhere. This is a pity, but then these are pitiful times, are they not?

Watch as Chapman plays around with the notion of chaos—and of order, too. First, he is not well pleased with what passes for democracy in the great republic. No anglophile, he does have a nice word or two for the British, in an essay that begins: "All good writing is the result of an acquaintance with the best books."[2] Chapman, like all of us who dwell in what Vice President Agnew once called "the greatest nation in the country," often feels obliged to invent the wheel each time he addresses his readers. He goes on: "But the mere reading of books will not suffice. Behind the books must lie the habit of unpremeditated, headlong conversation. We find that the great writers have been great talkers in every age."[3] He cites Shakespeare, as reported by Ben Jonson, Lord Byron, and our own Mark Twain. He then generalizes about other tribes, something now forbidden in the free world. He writes:

> The English have never stopped talking since Chaucer's time. And the other Europeans are ready-tongued, vocal, imaginative people, whose very folklore and early dialects, have been preserved by the ceaseless stream of talk on castled terraces and on village greens since Gothic times.
>
> But our democracy terrifies the individual, and our industrialism seals his lips. The punishment is very effective. It is simply this: "If you say such things as that, I won't play with you." Thus the average American goes about in quite a different humour from the average European, who is protected and fortified by his caste and clique, by his group and traditions, by manners and customs which are old and change slowly. The uniformity of the popular ideals and ambitions in America is at the bottom of most of our troubles. Industrialism has all but killed the English language among us, because every man is afraid

to make a joke—unless it be a stock joke. We are all as careful as diplomats not to show our claws. We wear white cotton gloves like waiters—for fear of leaving a thumb mark on the subject. Emerson's advice about this problem is covered by his apothegm, "If you are afraid to do any thing, do it!"[4]

Chapman on Plato:

Plato somewhere compares philosophy to a raft on which a shipwrecked sailor may perhaps reach home. Never was a simile more apt. Every man has his raft, which is generally large enough only for one. It is made up of things snatched from his cabin—a life preserver or two of psalm, proverb or fable; some planks held together by the oddest rope-ends of experience; and the whole shaky craft requires constant attention. How absurd, then, is it to think that any formal philosophy is possible—when the rag of old curtain that serves one man for a waistcoat is the next man's prayer-mat! To try to make a raft for one's neighbour, or try to get on to someone else's raft, these seem to be the besetting sins of philosophy and religion.

The raft itself is an illusion. We do not either make or possess our raft. We are not able to seize it or explain it, cannot summon it at will. It comes and goes like a phantom.[5]

As for Plato:

He was primarily an entertainer, a great impresario and setter of scenes, and stager of romances great and small where fact and fiction, religion and fancy, custom and myth are blended by imaginative treatment into—no one knows exactly what the mixture should be called.

The aim of his most elaborate work, the *Republic*, is identical with the aim of the Book of Job, of Bunyan's *Pilgrim's Progress*, of Milton's *Paradise Lost*, and indeed of half the great poems, plays and novels of the world, namely to justify the moral instinct.[6]

But Chapman is a literary critic as well as a moralist. He wrote:

> As a work of art, the *Republic* is atrocious, but as a garret-ful of antiquity it is thrilling. It is so cracked and rambling that Plato himself hardly knows what is in it. While clearing out a bureau drawer one day, he finds a clever little harangue denouncing sumptuary laws as both useless and foolish . . . "There's a glint of genius in that," says he and throws the manuscript into a big Sarcophagus labelled *Republic.*

Which is where, Chapman notes, it plainly does *not* belong, since Plato's entire work is based on the *necessity* of sumptuary laws.

> We see then what sort of a creature this Plato was—with his poetic gift, his inextinguishable moral enthusiasm, his enormous curiosity, his miscellaneous information, his pride of intellect and, as his greatest merit, his perception that spiritual truth must be conveyed indirectly and by allusions. In spite of certain clumsy dogmatisms to be found here and there in him, Plato knows that the assault upon truth cannot be carried by a frontal attack. It is the skirmishing of Plato which makes his thought carry; and all the labours of his expounders to reduce his ideas to a plain statement have failed. If the expounders could reduce Plato's meaning to a statement, Plato would be dead. He has had wit enough and vision enough to elude them all. His work is a province of romantic fiction, and his legitimate influence has been upon the romantic fiction and poetry of the world. Plato used Philosophy as a puppet on his stage, and made her convey thoughts which she is powerless to tell upon her own platform. He saw that philosophy

could live in the sea of moving fiction, but died on the dry land of formal statement. He was sustained in his art by the surrounding atmosphere of that Hellenic scepticism which adored elusiveness and hated affirmations. His age handed him his vehicle—to wit, *imaginary conversation*. Is there anything in the world that evaporates more quickly and naturally than conversation? But *imaginary* conversation! Certainly Plato has protected himself from cross-examination as well as ever man did. The cleverest pundits have been trying to edge him into the witness stand during sixty generations, but no one has ever cornered him. The street corner is his corner.[7]

Of Plato, as a voice from somewhere at the far edge of a democratic age, Chapman notes, with quiet pleasure, that:

It has thus become impossible for anyone to read Plato's dialogues or any other creation of the Greek brain with real sympathy; for those creations speak from a wonderful, cruel, remote, witty age, and represent the amusements of a wonderful, cruel, remote, witty people, who lived for amusement, and for this reason perished. Let us enjoy the playthings of this clever man but let us, so far as in us lies, forbear to cloy them with our explanations.[8]

Vico saw fit to systematize, if not to cloy, Plato in order to give us a useful overview of the evolution of human society, as glimpsed in the dark shadow of the cross of his day. It should be noted that Vico made far more of Plato's ideal theory than Plato did. But then, alas, Vico, like us, is serious and schematic.

Plato and Vico, Montesquieu and Jefferson, Margaret Thatcher and Ronald Reagan—the urge to devise model states is a constant and if chaos does not absolutely disintegrate us, we might yet endure as a race—if it is not a form of racism to suggest that human beings differ in *any* significant way from the mineral and the vegetable, two realms that we constantly victimize and are rude to.

Apropos of human political arrangements, I have been listening, lately, to a pair of voices from the century before ours; two voices often in harmony, more often in gentle dispute, I refer to Gustave Flaubert and George Sand. Put simply—too simply, I confess—George Sand was a nonromantic socialist while Flaubert was a romantic reactionary. Neither had much illusion about the perfectibility of man or too many notions as to the constitution of an ideal state. They wrote each other during the Franco-Prussian war, the collapse of the Second Empire, the rise of the Commune at Paris, and each wondered, "What next?"

Flaubert is glum: "Whatever happens, it will be a long time before we move forward again. Perhaps there's to be a recurrence of racial wars? Within a century we'll see millions of men kill each other at one go. All the East against all Europe, the old world against the new? Why not?"

Flaubert then teases George Sand:

The general reverence for universal suffrage revolts me more than the infallibility of the Pope. Do you think that if France, instead of being governed, in effect, by the mob, were to be ruled by the "Mandarins," we'd be where we are now? If only instead of wanting to enlighten the lower classes we had bothered to educate the upper classes![9]

Sand strikes back:

In my view, the vile experiment that Paris is undergoing in no way disproves the laws of eternal progress that govern both men and things, and if I have acquired any intellectual principles, good or bad, this business neither undermines nor alters them. A long time ago I accepted the necessity for patience in the same way as one accepts the weather, the long winter, old age, and failure in all its forms.[10]

Flaubert comes to the point: "I hate democracy (at least as it is understood in France), because it is based on 'the morality of the Gospels', which is immorality itself, whatever anyone may say: that is, the exaltation of Mercy at the expense of Justice, the negation of Right—the very opposite of social order."[11]

Sand remains serene: "I've never been able to separate the ideal of justice that you speak of from love: for if a natural society is to survive, its first law must be mutual service, as with the ants and the bees. In animals we call this collaboration of all to achieve the same end, instinct. The name doesn't matter. But in man, instinct is love, and whoever omits love omits truth *and* justice."[12]

"Tell me whether the tulip tree suffered from the frost this winter, and whether the peonies are doing well."[13]

That tulip tree may symbolize a benign way out of the current chaos. In the interest of shutting holes in the atmosphere, the human race may yet cooperate to survive, though I doubt it. For a new center to hold we must understand why it is that things fall apart the way they do. I have spent my life trying to understand what it was that so many others appear to need that I don't—specifically, a sense of deity, preferably singular, anthropomorphic, and, to explain the general mess of life that he has made on earth, an inscrutable jealous off-the-wall sort of god. I do not doubt that something new in this line is on its way but, meanwhile, there is something to be said for creative chaos. Certainly order, imposed from the top down, never holds for very long.

Like the rest of you, as the millennium is now ending, I keep thinking of how it began in Europe. Does a day pass that you do not give at least a fleeting thought to the Emperor

Otto III and to Pope Sylvester II? I should highly doubt it. After all, they are an attractive couple; a boy emperor and his old teacher, the intellectual pope. Together, at the start of our millennium, they decided to bring back the Christian empire that two centuries earlier Charlemagne had tried to recreate or—more precisely—to create among the warring tribes of western Europe. If Charlemagne was the Jean Monnet of the 800s, Otto III was the Jacques Delors of the 900s.[14] As you will recall, Otto was only fourteen when he became king of Germany. From boyhood, he took very seriously the idea of a united Christendom, a Holy Roman Empire. Like so many overactive, overeducated boys of that period he was a natural general, winning battles left and right in a Germany that rather resembled the China of Confucius's era—a time known as that of the warring duchies.

By sixteen, King Otto was crowned emperor of the West. An intellectual snob, he despised what he called "Saxon rusticity" and he favored what he termed Greek or Byzantine "subtlety." He even dreamed of sailing to Byzantium to bring together all Christendom under his rule, which was, in turn, under that of God. In all of this he was guided by his old tutor, a French scholar named Gerbert.

As a sign of solidarity—not to mention morbidity—Otto even opened up the tomb of Charlemagne and paid his great predecessor a visit. The dead emperor was seated on a throne. According to an eye witness, only a bit of his nose had fallen off, but his fingernails had grown through his gloves and so, reverently, Otto pared them and otherwise tidied him up. Can one imagine Delors—or even Helmut Kohl—doing as much for the corpse of Monnet?

Now we approach the fateful year 999. Otto is nineteen. He is obsessed with Italy, with Rome, with empire. In that year he sees to it that Gerbert is elected pope, taking the name Sylvester. Now emperor and pope move south to the decaying small town of Rome where Otto builds himself a palace on the Aventine—a bad luck hill, as Cicero could have testified.

Together, Otto and Sylvester lavished their love and their ambition upon the Romans, who hated both of them with a passion. In the year that our common millennium properly began, 1001, the Romans drove emperor and pope out of the city. Otto died at twenty-two in Palermo, of smallpox. A year later, Sylvester was dead, having first, it is said, invented the organ. Thus, the dream of a European union ended in disaster for the two dreamers.

I will not go so far as to say that the thousand years since Otto's death have been a total waste of time. Certainly, other dreamers have had similar centripetal dreams. But those centrifugal forces that hold us in permanent thrall invariably undo the various confederacies, leagues, empires, thousand-year-old reichs that the centripetalists would impose upon us from the top down.

Some years ago I had a lively exchange here at an Oxford political club. I had remarked that the nation state, as we know it, was the nineteenth-century invention of Bismarck when he united the German tribes in order to beat the Franks, and of Lincoln in North America when he deprived of all significant power our loosely federated states in favor of a mystical highly centralized union. A not so kindly don instructed me that, as *everyone* knows, the nation state was the result of the Thirty Years War and the treaty of Westphalia. I said that I was aware that that was indeed the received opinion, which he had been hired to dispense, but it was plain to me that the forceful bringing together of disparate peoples against their will and imposing on them universal education— to make them like-minded and subservient—as well as military conscription, signified the end of one sort of democratic era, to advert to Vico's triad, and the beginning of our modern unwieldy and, for their unhappy residents, most onerous nation states.

What is happening today in the old Soviet Union and Yugoslavia—as well as the thousand-and-one rebellions of subject tribes against master tribes—seems to me a very good thing if we are able to draw the right lesson from all this turbulence. Thanks to CNN and other television networks, we follow, day by day, at least one or two of the thousand or so wars for "freedom" that are simultaneously being fought as worn-out centralized political structures collapse. Instead of wringing our hands and dreaming dreams of a peaceful world order centered upon Brussels or Strasbourg, why not accept the fact that if people want to separate they should be allowed to? The sky will not fall in. In due course, the Muslim states of the southern tier of the old Soviet Union may want to come together in some sort of loose trade and cultural and, alas, religious federation. Why oppose them? Western Europe has already gone about as far as it needs to go toward unification. A common currency will mean a common tax collector, which will mean a common police force, which will mean tyranny in the long run and a lot of time wasted in the short run. Despite the Norwegians' insistence on giving peace prizes to the wrong people, they are not entirely stupid when it comes to their common good.

The dream of Otto and Sylvester, if ever made even partial reality, will hasten a new theocratic age, which will promptly become imperial thanks to modern technology. The world could then, most easily, become a prison for us all and with no world elsewhere to escape to.

Great centrifugal forces are at work all around the earth and why resist them? For the centripetally minded—theocratic or imperial or both—the mosaic of different tribes that will occupy Europe from homely Bantry to glittering Vladivostok are bound to come together in the interest of mundane trade. Is not that quite enough? At least in the absence of a new god.

Certainly, there is greater safety for the individual in a

multitude of states where the citizen is computerized, as it were, upon a tape, than there can possibly be in any vast centralized state. Although the United States is only a middling-size country, it is often at the so-called cutting edge when it comes to the very latest technologies of control. Recently a government spokesman noted that by the year 2008 there will be a central computer that will contain everyone's financial dealings, including bank balances, use of credit cards, and so on. At the touch of a button, the Treasury will know who has what money and the Treasury will then be able to deduct what it thinks it may need in the way of tax. "The power to tax; the power to destroy," as Emerson is said to have said.

Meanwhile, total control over all of the people all of the time is the traditional aim of almost every government. In earlier times, this was only a tyrant's dream. Now it is technically possible. And has any technology ever *not* been put to use? We are told that democracy is a safeguard against misuse of power. I wouldn't know. I have never lived in a democracy. There are several near-democracies in Europe, small countries like Denmark, Holland, Switzerland, small relatively homogeneous—or, like Switzerland, ingeniously balanced heterogeneous—populations that are able to put important issues immediately to the people through referenda. Large states cannot or will not do this. Certainly no serious attempt to create a democracy has ever been made in the United States—and now it is far too late in the day for us. At least Great Britain has never gone around proclaiming itself a model democracy as we have done. Even so, I am only able to present this essay because both the United Kingdom and the United States still cling to ameliorative liberal traditions that keep us from being entirely totalitarian, even if we are not entirely—or even adequately—free as citizens or subjects.

John Adams proudly proclaimed that Americans would have a government not of men but of laws. We have; but *what* laws!

There are young men and women in prison for life for having been caught a third time with marijuana. Thanks to the criminalizing of so many areas of human activity from drugs to sex we have more than one million people in prison and over two million on parole or probation. Our prisons are the scandal of the first world and should certainly be investigated in depth by Amnesty, which usually prefers to complain about crimes against humanity in Ulan Bator rather than those committed by our own people against our own people at home. Far more men are raped each year in the American prison system than are women on the outside. But no one cares. A state with too many laws becomes, in effect, law-less, mind-less, and heart-less.

For those interested in how to control an entire population, we have invented a magnetic bracelet, which is worn, tastefully, on wrist or ankle, thus making it possible for a central guardian to keep track of the bracelet's movements. At first, the European union will use this jewelry to keep track of aliens; then possible criminals; then. . . . We have surpassed Orwell's rather innocent imaginings.

As you may gather, I hate the nation state as it has been evolving in my time and now looks to be metastasizing in all of Europe and, perhaps, parts of Asia. I am literally a grandchild of the American Civil War, and I belonged to the losing side. Had the issue of that war been the abolition of slavery, I could not have faulted our defeat—morally at least. But Mr. Lincoln—the first of the modern tyrants—chose to fight the war not on the issue of slavery but on the holiness and indivisibility of a union that he alone had any understanding of. With his centralizing of all power at Washington this "reborn" [sic] union[15] was ready for a world empire that has done us as little good as it has done the world we have made so many messes in.

I live part of each year in Italy, which is not, properly speaking, a state at all as many Italians are beginning to note, some wistfully, some angrily. Devolution is very much in the air on the Italian peninsula. Why should the capital of Savoy be at Rome and not where it has always been at Turin? It is my impression that most of the old Italian city states—and some larger entities—would like autonomy within a loose trade federation centered on Brussels—or anywhere except Rome. The region from which the Vidals came to America—the Veneto, Friuli, southern Tirol—has recently asked to be excused from the Italian republic. This universal centrifugal force is now the central fact of world politics. Why does any government stand in its way? The answer is stupidly simple. Rulers like to have lots of subjects. They like a large tax base. They enjoy showing off to one another. When Bismarck introduced universal education for all children whether the parents wanted it or not, each empire was then able to use the educational system to promote patriotism and obedience to the status quo, which meant fighting, usually as conscripts, in any war that looked financially appealing to the rulers.

Thanks to television, one interesting development is that in those rare cases when we are allowed to see firsthand oppression by Serbs or by Russians or by Israelis, the viewer is jolted by what is being done not only to civilian victims but to the young soldiers that the masters of the nation states have sent into battle, often, at least in the case of Russia, without sufficient training or motivation. Even the American empire, with its mercenary armed forces, does not dare engage in too long or too bloody a war after Vietnam. Our television viewers do not easily tolerate the deaths—on film—of young Americans in far-off lands. It was the unexpected genius of George Bush to pull off a war in the Persian Gulf—with the collusion of television—in order to minimize American casualties (few in any case) and obscure Iraqi casualties in the tens of thousands. But that sort of controlled war is rare and hugely expensive. For now, in areas where the West is either not greatly concerned or helpless to act, we are shown the horrors of war, or pestilence, or famine. But when these things come too close to home, the screen goes blank.

Recently, I did a documentary for British television on my home city of Washington, D.C. I was particularly intrigued by the opportunity to show, for the first time on television, the black city of Washington, some seven hundred thousand people at whose center is a well-guarded gilded ghetto known, without irony, as the capital of the free world. The race war between white masters and black helots goes on and on. Drugs are trafficked promiscuously and the city delights in the knowledge that it may well be the murder capital of the Western world. The documentary had an excellent director who went out to the Anacostia Flats where Calcutta-like living conditions obtain. I got the black leader Jesse Jackson to talk to me, on camera, about the problems of his people in their city. I must say I was looking forward to the result. This should be an eye-opener, I thought, for Americans—and they are, after all, the people that concern me most.

When I saw the film, to my amazement there was no Jesse Jackson, no Anacostia Flats. Instead, there were meaningless shots of the president, coming and going, and crowds, and funerals, and incoherent mention of a high murder rate but no explanation why.

What happened? The producers wanted to sell the film to the United States, as did I. The Public Broadcasting System is the logical place for it to be shown. But PBS is partially funded by Congress and Congress is now in the hands of the anti-black faction of our single-party system. So the program was censored—by itself, I should think. We are allowed to know the worst about Russians against the Chechens but we cannot hear the Reverend Jackson tell us that in a country that freed itself from England on the one line "No taxation without representation," seven hundred thousand residents of the District of Columbia are not allowed to elect one of their own to that Congress which presides over their city and collects their tax money.

Now I notice that elements of the British Labour Party are discussing devolution for Scotland and Wales—I dare not mention Ireland in any context. Since no one anywhere much cares for Westminster or Whitehall why not let Edinburgh, say, make its own arrangements with the Common Market, bypassing the Southeast.

Europeans think, rather smugly, that they are not given to such primitive Christianity as Americans, but this is wishful thinking. In bad times who knows what terrible gods will emerge from under the flat rocks of this old continent that has given the world so much mindless savagery in the twentieth century alone.

Let pluralism and diversity be our aim. There is already more than enough union, through international cartels, which pay no nation loyalty much less tax, and through television, which is better off in the hands of numerous minor states than it can ever be as the "public" television of any great united state.

Should a theocratic age be upon us—and certainly fundamentalist Christians, Jews, and Muslims have never been busier—then the larger the political entity, the greater the danger for that administrative unit the citizen. Currently, in the United States, militant Jesus-Christers are organizing in order to take political control not only at the local level but at that of the Congress itself. This is disturbing.

In the last century a Speaker of the American House of Representatives was so reactionary that it was said of him that if God had consulted him about creation, he would have voted for chaos. Considering the alternatives, for now at least, so would I.

DISSIDENCE AND CREATIVITY

Nawal El Saadawi

I started writing this paper on January 1, 1995. I wrote it in English though my language is Arabic and my country is Egypt. I was born in Egypt and have lived there almost all my life, but for the last two years I have been teaching at Duke University as a visiting professor. I hope to be back in Egypt in 1996. All my books, whether fiction or nonfiction, are written in Arabic and are published and read in Egypt and other countries of the Arab world. When I am faced with censorship in Egypt I publish my work in Lebanon or another Arab country. This context is important for me when I try to understand what we mean by dissidence or by the dissident word.

Today I will be speaking about the intrinsic dissidence of the creative word, and the languages of imperialism and oppression that authors have forged into instruments of liberation. But it is difficult for me to do that without speaking in Arabic, difficult for me to be creative both in mind and body when using a foreign tongue. What I am doing now is translating my Arabic into English. When I do that, a part of the meaning is lost or changed. But although my English is different from the English you use here and may have its defects, it expresses me better than if I had given my lecture to an English translator.

I: What Is Dissidence?

I have tried to find the Arab word for dissidence. In Arabic we say protest (*al-ihtijaj*), or opposition (*al-mu'arada*), or disputation/litigation (*al-mukhasama*), or to rebel (*yatamarradu*), or to revolt (*yathuru*). But each of these words has a different meaning according to the context in which the dissidence or struggle takes place. For me the word *struggle* in Arabic (*al-nidal*) sheds most light on the meaning of dissidence. The *dissident* in Arabic (*al-munadil*) means the fighter who cooperates with others to struggle against oppression and exploitation, whether personal or political.

I believe there is no dissidence without struggle. We cannot understand dissidence except in a situation of struggle and in its location in place and time. Without this, dissidence becomes a word devoid of responsibility, devoid of meaning.

II: Demystifying Words

Can I be dissident without being creative? Can I have the passion and knowledge required to change the powerful oppressive system of family and government without being creative? What do we mean by creativity? Can we be creative if we obey others or follow the tradition of our ancestors? Can we be creative if we submit to the rules forced upon us under different names: father, God, husband, family, nation, security, stability, protection, peace, democracy, family planning, development, human rights, modernism, or postmodernism?

These fifteen terms are used globally and locally by both the oppressors and the oppressed. I chose them because we read or hear them all the time, whether we live in Egypt, the United States, Brazil, or India. They constitute a large part of the language of imperialism and oppression. But they are often used by the oppressed in a different meaning, in the fight against imperialism and oppression.

For example the word *protection* seems a very positive word. British colonialism in Egypt was inaugurated by a military occupation in 1882.[1] It hindered our economic and cultural development for more than seventy years. Instead of having the freedom to develop our agriculture to satisfy our needs, we were obliged to produce cotton for the needs of British industry. The result was increasing poverty in Egypt and increasing wealth in Britain. This was done in the name of protection, not of colonialism or exploitation. The British used military power and terrorism to achieve these ends. The rulers of Egypt, the khedives, submitted to British power.[2] The royal family and the ruling class collaborated with the colonizers to protect their joint interests. Egyptians who challenged the government or the British were labelled dissidents, communists, or nationalists, and were killed, imprisoned, dismissed from their work, or forced to live in exile or starvation.

Today the neocolonizers do not use the word protection anymore. The colonized people in Egypt, Africa, India, and elsewhere have seen through it. The word protection was demystified through people's living experience; protection to us in Egypt now means colonialism. Another word therefore had to be used by the neocolonizers. It had to be just as positive and innocent, but more progressive. So the word *development* came into use in the early seventies. Many people in Egypt and other so-called developing countries were deceived by this word, but the results of development proved to be even more pernicious than the results of protection.

Much more money traveled from the developing countries (or third world) to the first world than in the opposite direction. The gap between the rich and poor increased both locally and globally. Even the United Nations Organization could not hide these facts. They appeared in statistics and in UN reports written by field workers in Africa, Asia, and Latin America.

In 1979 I was one of the UN field workers in Ethiopia. I worked with the UN for two years, then I left. I discovered that development projects promoted by the UN and Western corporations and agencies hindered development in Egypt and Africa. They were a disguised form of economic genocide, more pernicious than military genocide because they killed more people but were not as visible as blood shed in war.

When the word development was demystified the neocolonizers shifted their terms. The new term is *structural adjust-*

ment, now being promoted by the World Bank. Few people understand this word. But when structural adjustment is implemented in Africa and other parts of the so-called South, the effect is no different from that of protection or development. The result is even greater poverty in the poor South, and greater riches for the rich North. To name just one example: from 1984 to 1990 Structural Adjustment Policies (SAPs) led to the transfer of US$178 billion from the South to the commercial banks in the North.

Another neocolonial word is *aid.* It is another myth that is becoming demystified. Many countries in the South have started to raise the slogan: Fair Trade Not Aid. Here is one example from Egypt: between 1975 (when American aid to Egypt began) and 1986, Egypt imported commodities and services from the U.S. to a total of US$30 billion. During the same period Egypt exported to the U.S. commodities worth only US$5 billion.

Egyptians who stand up and challenge the global neocolonialist powers and their collaborators in local governments are labelled dissident, communist, nationalist, or feminist. They are punished according to the effectiveness of their dissidence; this ranges from losing their job and censorship of their writings, to prison and even death.

In Egypt, under Sadat, we had to demystify some of the words and slogans he used. One of his slogans was The Open Door Policy. It proved to be no more than opening the doors to a neocolonial assault on the economy of Egypt and its culture. American products (Coca Cola, cigarettes, nylon clothes, McDonald's, makeup, TV programs, films, and so on) invaded Egypt, destroying local production. Sadat inaugurated his rule with what he described as a "corrective revolution." The corrective revolution in fact was no more than a correction in the flow of money to ensure that it ended up in the pockets of the ruling groups that came to power after Nasser's death in 1970.

III: Mutual Responsibility

Our struggles are becoming more and more difficult. They need more and more creativity. There are always new words emerging that we have to demystify, words such as: peace, democracy, human rights, privatization, globalization, multiculturalism, diversity, civil society, nongovernmental organizations (NGOs), cultural difference, liberation theology, religious fundamentalism, postmodernism, and others. We need to discover new ways of exposing the paradoxes or double meanings in the many new and old words that are endlessly repeated. This needs greater knowledge and more understanding of modern and postmodern techniques of oppression and exploitation.

We cannot acquire this knowledge through books, through formal education or the mass media. All of them are controlled by the global and local powers of domination and exploitation, and they help to veil our brains with one myth after another. We have to acquire this knowledge by ourselves, from our own experience in the daily struggle against those powers globally, locally, and in the family. This is creativity. It is inspired and stimulated by our living our own lives and not by copying theories of struggle from books.

Every struggle has its own unique theory inseparable from action. Creativity means uniqueness: innovation. Discovering new ways of thinking and acting, of creating a system based on more and more justice, freedom, love, and compassion. If you are creative, you must be dissident. You discover what others have not yet discovered. You may be alone at the beginning, but somehow you feel responsible toward yourself and others; toward those who are not yet aware of this discovery, who share your struggle with the system; toward those who have lost hope and have submitted.

Can there be any struggle or dissidence without responsibility toward oneself and others? Is there any human who does not struggle against oppression? We are all born dissidents to a greater or a lesser degree. But during the last two years I have ceased to consider myself a dissident. I have been a dissident since childhood. My name was put on the Egyptian government's black list in 1962. I had to face censorship. I lost my job in 1972, our health association and magazine were banned in 1973. In 1981, I was put in jail and in 1991 our women's association, AWSA (Arab Women's Solidarity Association), and magazine *Noon* were banned. In 1992, my life was threatened and security guards were placed around my house.

Now I am a visiting professor in Duke University in the United States. I teach creativity and dissidence to students. But can you really teach these things? All you can do is to open up closed doors; undo what education did; encourage students to discover their own dissidence in their own lives.

IV: Dissidence and Distance

I watch what is happening in Egypt from a distance. In November 1994, floods in upper Egypt left thousands of people homeless. I received a letter from a young woman student, who lives in Cairo. Her family lives in a village in Luxor (one of the places hit by the floods). She said:

> I went to visit my family and my village when I heard about the floods. Thank God my father and mother survived but they were left with no home, no shelter. The authorities were busy with a big tourist show, busy preparing to mount the opera *Aida*, in front of the Temple of Hatshepsut. Priority was given to satisfying the needs of American tourists and not the homeless thousands. Each tourist sat on a blanket to warm his seat while he was watching the show. My family received no blankets to

sleep in the cold nights. They lost their cane sugar farm because the local authorities took it over together with other farms to build roads and bridges for tourists, so that they could reach Hatshepsut's Temple easily. Four hundred acres of cane sugar were taken by force from homeless people. Other farms were taken from people to secure a space around the open *Aida* stadium (a security belt to protect the tourists from the so-called fundamentalists). The average yield of each acre is 50 tons, the price of each ton is 90 pounds constituting a loss of about 2 million pounds to the people. Two other bridges were built on Asjun canal for tourists to cross on their way to the show, and more farms were taken from people. This will result in an acute drop in the local production of cane sugar. An American company called Orascom built the bridges and the stadium in collaboration with Onsy Saweeris who opened a McDonald's eating place as well. The waters of the flood were quickly pumped out of the graves and temples of the dead pharaohs. The local authorities were boasting to the tourists that the waters did not spend one night in Siti the First Temple in Korana, or rather, that Siti the First did not sleep one night in the waters. But thousands of homeless people were left to the floods with no shelter. In front of the Karnak temple there was another big tourist show. One thousand five hundred girls and boys danced for one month and half. Each one of them received ten pounds. The police were everywhere to protect the tourists and the dancers. The fundamentalists are against music shows and dances. The tourists call them terrorists. But the tourists are terrorists too. They frightened everybody, even the local authorities, who were so afraid of the fundamentalists that they destroyed hundreds of cane sugar farms.

They said that the fundamentalists used these cane sugar farms as hiding places. My father and mother are among these people. I do not know how I can help them. I have to go to Cairo and let a friend of mine who is a journalist in *Ruz al-yusif* magazine write about it. Our government does not help anybody unless the journalists write about them, or the TV or CNN broadcast something about their story. During the population conference in Cairo last September, the CNN showed something about female circumcision. After that everybody in the government and in the media was speaking about female circumcision. Even the Mufti, the highest Islamic authority in Egypt, wrote in *Ruz al-Yusif* opposing this operation. The Sheik of Al-Azhar also wrote in the same magazine, but he supported the operation and said that it is an Islamic duty. I will send you a copy of this issue. It was published on 17 October 1994. I hope that the government listens to the Mufti and prohibits the circumcision of girls, but the government is afraid of the fundamentalists, who force the people to circumcise their girls and to veil them.

After the show of *Aida* people caught an old tourist with a girl dancer hiding in Karnak temple. The girl was veiled. The tourist was very drunk and he told the people that he is more excited by the veil than by belly dancing.

The fundamentalists are becoming more and more harsh on girls and women. They prevent them from going out even to school. They tell the girls that they are protecting them from being raped by tourists.

In the Cairo International Population Conference I met a young woman in the AWSA workshop. I was glad to know from her that you have started an AWSA branch in North America. Her name is Amina Ayad. She read the paper you prepared on AWSA. It made me aware of the fact that increasing poverty in Egypt is due to the development forced on us by the West rather than the high fertility of Egyptian women.

I used to come to the AWSA weekly seminars and to read *Noon* magazine. I met you many times. You may remember my face but you do not know my name. I was not a member of AWSA but I was very sad when the government banned it in Egypt in 1991. I read in *Al-ahali* that you have taken the government to court. But the court is part of the government. I have no hope in this government. Nobody is helping my father and mother. I have to leave them and go back to my school in Cairo. I took your address in America from Amina Ayad. She told me that she met you in the University of Washington. You may know someone in the CNN who can broadcast something about my family in Luxor. If this happens the government will hurry up and build them a home or a shelter or at least give them blankets. It is very cold at night in Luxor, more cold than Cairo. I am crying while writing to you.

In Durham, I am ten thousand miles from Egypt and from women and men whose struggles I have shared: against British colonialism, Egyptian governments, neocolonialism, fanatical religious and political groups, the oppressive family code, and other forms of oppression in our private and public lives. In Durham I look at my country from a distance. Sometimes I lose hope. But we cannot be dissidents without hope. We cannot be dissidents from a distance or if we are not in the struggle. When we struggle we do not lose hope. We feel responsible toward ourselves and the others.

V: Intellectual Terrorism

The relation between self and other becomes simple and clear when we struggle, but it becomes very complex, very vague, very difficult to understand when we read books or listen to lectures, especially by so-called postmodern philosophers. It becomes a puzzle or conundrum. We find ourselves lost in an avalanche of words that appear very dissident, and that multiply and reproduce themselves endlessly, breeding more and more complex words. We drown in these words, we are suffocated by them. It is a zero-sum game of words in which you lose your power to understand.

In spring 1994, a friend of mine, a South American scholar at a U.S. university, attended a conference at Duke University at which Jacques Derrida had been invited to lecture. He was very attentive during Derrida's lecture but understood very little. He felt frustrated and did not have the courage to ask questions. When others asked a question, the answer complicated matters. That night, he had a nightmare: Derrida's fingers were around his neck trying to suffocate him. The nightmare was of course unreal, but this does not mean that it was insignificant. It had symbolic truth for the person who suffered it. Another friend of mine, an American scholar, attended the same lecture. He considered it a dissident postmodern lecture. The South American scholar discussed it with him and became even more frustrated. He felt the lecture was an act of intellectual terrorism.

In November 1994 I found myself sitting in a huge solemn hall, listening to men and women scholars, the women with big earrings, very red lips, and thick makeup, the men wearing neckties, their fingernails manicured, smelling of aftershave and deodorants, their teeth and shoes shining in the electric light. Some of them are well known in the United States and Europe. They are not known to the majority of people who live in Africa, Asia, or Latin America, or even to the people in their own countries who do not read books. But they call themselves global scholars or international philosophers.

Their language was so dry, so complicated, that the huge hall full of young students seeking knowledge was almost empty after the first session. These scholars drowned in abstract theories and words taken out of context. They sometimes used Marxist ideas about capitalism and imperialism. They criticized the separation of economies from culture. But this was only a philosophical judgment that was quickly forgotten in order to adopt other ideas from Foucault or Derrida and again distinguish between the cultural and the political or the social and the economic.

They spoke about the responsibility of the intellectual toward oppressed people in the third world, whom they called the "subaltern," the "docile bodies," or the "subject." We, the people in the so-called third world were reduced to bodies (docile or not), we were decapitated just as happened to women in the name of God in the three monotheistic religions. But then they forgot these ideas and solemnly announced the death of the intellectual, looking furtively around as though suspicious of whether they, the intellectuals, still existed and still had a function.

As usual, they quoted Michel Foucault and Gilles Deleuze's phrases: "Those who act and struggle are no longer represented either by a group or union that appropriates their right to stand as their conscience."[3] Once more they used this paradoxical statement that could mean one of two contradictory things: 1) the end of the role of intellectuals who replace the language of struggling people with their own language— this is a positive interpretation since it is aimed at liberating the voice of the oppressed and thus empowering them—or 2) disempowering oppressed people by divorcing their struggle from the struggle of other groups or collectivities.

Here the word struggle is itself ambiguous. It can be a genuinely dissident word if struggle means action and not just words to be replaced by other words that do not change the systems of oppression and exploitation at any level. Struggle is both action-thinking and speaking out. There is no separation between the practice and the theory of struggle. But these simple ideas were totally absent in the conference.

Here also responsibility toward the self and the other is transformed into a conundrum, since the struggling/dissident creative person, who has acquired new knowledge or demystified certain myths, can, it is said, no longer represent the struggle of his or her group. In the same way I might say that "groups or unions" are formed out of a nonfragmented struggle and this, too, might be just empty words. On the other hand, it might equally refer to a progressive idea, that of liberating those who struggle from the power of the leading dissident: the so-called hero.

VI: Dissidence and Heroism

The creative dissident is not a hero or heroine. He or she should be the first to be killed in the battle. The concept of heroism or leadership differs from that of dissidence. In battles the leader is often the last to be killed, while unknown soldiers are shot at the front. The dissident is not a hero or leader. The hero is worshipped as a demigod, but the dissident is punished and cursed like Satan (*Iblis* in Arabic). The devil is responsible for what is called evil. Since the evolution of monotheism, Satan has become the symbol of dissidence, of disruption of the existing order.

The devil is responsible for disasters, defeat, and misery. But the devil has no power relative to God. Though God has all the power, he is not responsible for any disaster, defeat, or misery. The split between power and responsibility has lain at the core of oppression and exploitation from the advent of slavery to this day. Dissidence is the antithesis of power divorced from responsibility for the misery of people. Responsibility does not mean aid or charity; it means trying to eradicate the causes of poverty and oppression. The concept of charity or aid is as pernicious to others as the concept of replacing the other's language or mind.

For creative dissidence does not believe in the dichotomy "god-devil" or "self-other." Both are to be challenged and criticized equally. This means directing a critical gaze at the self as well as at the other.

If we wanted to translate these ideas into postmodern language, we might say that the deheroization of self and other is at the core of real dissidence: of radical ethics, an aesthetics of creativity, or a critical ontology of self and other. Real dissidence avoids lapsing into the reverse essentialism of a cult of self or the other. It also avoids one-way reflexive self-monitoring by including the other in this process. It is thus that the analytical links between ourselves and our social context are maintained.

VII: Dissidence and Fundamentalism

Radicalism is a part of creative dissidence. But postmodernists do not question the established canon of neocolonial economico-politico-cultural imperialism. They do not question the hegemony of male philosophers in the so-called first world, of male gods and male prophets. They limit themselves to cultural imperialism: to the problems of power/knowledge and of self-knowledge and identity. This established philosophical canon began with the patriarchal slave or class system and is still prevalent today.

Fundamentalism, like radicalism, is a positive and original way of thinking necessary to any creative dissident work. But both of them have come to be labelled negatively, like communism, socialism, and feminism.

Individual identity or individual responsibility is inseparable from social identity or social responsibility, and the word identity is a positive word, like democracy and freedom. But these words are all used by neocolonialists to obstruct the freedom or identity of the others, to favor the development of so-called modern or postmodern democratic free societies.

So we find that concepts like radical ethics, religious freedom, liberation theology, and cultural autonomy have not led to greater freedom or to fundamental cultural and economic changes that improve our lives. They have led to what is now called religious fundamentalism and fanatical spiritual movements using religion or culture to abolish the other (the devil). These fanatical religions and political movements are spreading all over the world. Christian, Jewish, Islamic, Buddhist, or Hindu, they have become very prominent in many regions.

Postmodernism itself is a form of cultural fundamentalism. It is the other face of religious fundamentalism. Both are products of neocolonialism. Perhaps we would do better to name them pseudomodernism and pseudofundamentalism since they both function and combine to maintain the global capitalist system.

The concepts that we have mentioned are new forms of imperialism, terrorism, and tourism: they make use of indigenous culture or religion as a tool to serve their own economic and intellectual interests. Philosophical imperialism and its discourse are inseparable from cultural and economic imperialism.

Here is just one example from Egypt: In 1994, the U.S. government threatened to cut off so-called U.S. aid to Egypt if a law was not promulgated to protect U.S. films and cultural products. The Egyptian ministry of culture was obliged to draft a new law under the title "Protection of Intellectual Rights." This law will apply only to U.S. "cultural" products.[4] The Egyptian government was not able to resist U.S. government pressure on this issue. Yet few in Egypt still believe in the mystique of U.S. aid. The problem is not only one of demystifying or acquiring new knowledge. It is a question of economic, political, military, and cultural power.

Knowledge is power. But the power of knowledge alone is not enough in a world where military power can intervene at any moment to protect the economic interests of neocolonialists, as it did in the Gulf War or Somalia under slogans like "human rights," "democracy," "humanitarian aid."

The American government is using the postmodern General Agreement on Tariffs and Trade (GATT agreement) signed in Uruguay in 1993 to impose cultural imperialism on people everywhere: in Africa, Asia, Latin America, the Arab countries, Russia, Eastern and Western Europe. American cultural products (films, TV programs, books, and music) have become a profitable export industry in the so-called free market—almost as profitable as the trade in arms; almost as profitable as the trade in beauty products for women: big earrings, makeup, and even oriental veils for those who want to be exotic or choose what they call their authentic Muslim identity.

But the free market is being demystified rapidly, being exposed as the freedom of the powerful to exploit the less powerful. In the year 1994, everybody in Egypt was talking about the Bad Meat Scandal.[5] The European Community threatened to obstruct the sale of Egyptian exports because the Egyptian government was not being flexible enough to disregard the most elementary health rules for imported meat. These prescribe that fat content should not exceed 20 percent and that the expiry date should be respected. Large amounts of bad meat, in which the fat content reached 35 percent or more, were imported into Egypt, threatening the health of thousands of people. Often the expiry date was almost due. This kind of meat is fed to pigs and other animals in European countries since it is no longer suitable for human consumption.

This kind of pressure is exerted in the name of freedom of the market. Nonflexible governments in the third world are considered bad or "dissident" governments. The global neo-colonial powers are able to punish them in ways corresponding to their level of "dissidence" or "inflexibility." Punishment includes the threat of economic or military sanctions and of defamation: publicizing their human rights violations in the global media.

The United Nations and human rights organizations are often an instrument in this neocolonial game. In the same way the so-called nongovernmental organizations or movements in "civil society" have become new instruments to out-flank local governments that are still sufficiently powerful and organized to put up some resistance.

"Privatization," "nongovernmental organizations," or "civil society" are all considered positive terms for men and women who are fighting against local dictators and oppressive governments. But in the hands of neocolonialists, they are transformed into swords directed against local people. Swords and words are used to divide the people in the name of diversity, while the neocolonialists globalize in NATO or in transnational corporations (TNCs).

This is a game in which God has all the power of both word and sword and is always the winner, while the devil—ourselves—is the loser. The devil is dissident and the angels are docile, obedient, tolerant, moderate, and flexible groups and individuals.

In 1991, our NGO, the Arab Women's Solidarity Association in Egypt, was banned by the government. The AWSA was considered locally and globally a dissident group. Why? Because we did not distinguish between patriarchy and neocolonialism, and we protested against the Gulf War. But how can women, who are half the population, be liberated in countries that are neither economically nor culturally liberated?

Our concepts in AWSA emerged from our experience as women struggling against all kinds of oppression exercised in the name of God, the father, the husband, the state, the United Nations, or international law.

VIII: Dissident Philosophers

The word *philosophy* in Arabic is *al-falsafa*. There are important Arab philosophers, but most of their work is in Arabic and the most important parts of their work have not been translated or studied in the West. Many Western scholars think that philosophy, like feminism, is a Western invention. People who read history think that philosophy started with the Greeks. This idea is related to nineteenth-century colonialism. Egyptian history is reduced to what is called Egyptology, to stones and ruins looked at by tourists.

Colonialism uses military terrorism and cultural tourism at the same time. Cameras in the hands of tourists are like guns in the hands of colonialists, like pens in the hands of postmodernists. The upshot is words in books or images on the TV screen about "clean" neocolonial wars, whether physical, economic, or cultural.

Egyptology is an example of cultural genocide or terrorism, in which a whole nation and its civilization and philosophy are violently reduced to a few stones or ruins. Egyptian philosophers have disappeared from history. One of them was a woman philosopher called Hypatia. She was killed twice: the first time in A.D. 415 by foreign invaders who killed her physically and burned her books together with the whole library of Alexandria in Egypt.[6] The second time was in the nineteenth century when she was assassinated culturally and historically by the Egyptologists.

Not all philosophers are, like Hypatia, killed because of what they write or think. That depends on the effectiveness of their dissidence or challenge to the political system that rules over them. If a philosopher produces many works that change nothing in the power system because they do not reach people and are not understood, he or she may remain safe and secure, even prosperous. The dissident word must be effective in real life, otherwise it loses its meaning and is no longer dissident. Thinking that is isolated from real life is not part of the struggle. The dissident word is an expression of a struggling woman or man whose body and mind and spirit are inseparable. Can you have a dissident mind and a docile body or a cold heart? A dissident writer is both a philosopher and an activist.

Philosophers who are not activists in a struggle end up as empty shells: as shelves of books in academia. They struggle in closed rooms, using words to fence with other users of words. They have a love-hate relationship with poor oppressed women and men who are struggling to live. They worship them, call them the subaltern, glorify their authentic identity or culture, but at the same time look down on them, consider them as docile or struggling bodies unable to produce philosophy, or as local activists but not global thinkers. They abolish subaltern philosophies and replace them on the global intellectual scene; they become the philosophers of the subaltern who knows more about them than the subaltern know about themselves.

IX: Tourism and Postmodernism

There are important similarities between tourists and postmodernists. Both appear to be physically present in nature, but in fact they are empty shells: ghosts haunting what are called cultural differences. Both consume cultural differences, diversity, multiculturalism, authenticity, creativity, and even dissidence. For them indigenous people do not exist. They have become a piece of stone, a collection of images, words, and symbols, an abstraction or nature-culture.

Both postmodernists and tourists consume the other or use the other as a tool for consumption. To them everything (including the subaltern) becomes a commodity to be used materially, culturally, or intellectually. Multiculturalism, diversity, cultural difference, religious difference, ethnic difference, authenticity, specificity are the new commodities. The postmodernists even go back to glorifying blood relations, feudal patriarchal family ties, and tribal societies. Like pagans they worship the gods or statues that they have created out of stone or words or images.

I have seen tourists in Egypt kiss the stone of the pyramid in Giza like pilgrims kissing the black stone in Mecca. In my village in the delta of the Nile, an American woman scholar kissed a veiled girl and praised her veil as a sign of her authentic identity. Another American woman scholar produced a film about subaltern or Egyptian women who are going back to the veil, back to their authentic culture. She praised the veil in her film and said: "Nowadays Egyptian women have their own revolution and are not imitating Western women." The title of her film was *A Veiled Revolution*(!). She is considered an expert on Middle Eastern culture, and has the money and equipment needed to produce such films. We Egyptian women are considered ignorant of our culture. We have to be guided by American experts. They mediate our experience for us and then sell back to us their image of ourselves.

The veil is forced on Egyptian women by religio-political groups. It is no different culturally from the postmodern veil made of cosmetics and hair dyes that is forced on Western women by the media and beauty commercials. In an international women's conference, a French woman scholar said the veil was linked to Islam. I mentioned that veiling preceded Islam, and existed in both Christianity and Judaism, that it in fact arose with the slave system. She said, "I am Christian but I am not veiled." While she was speaking I noticed that she had a thick coating of makeup on her face. She was not aware that she herself was also wearing a veil. This postmodern veil is seen by the global neocolonial media as beautiful, feminine, a sign of progress, though it is as pernicious to the humanity and authentic identity of the woman who wears it as the so-called religious veil.

X: The Dissident God

In another conference an Arab scholar tried to glorify his culture, his religion, his Islam, by proving that women in Islamic societies could be heads of government, as they now are in Pakistan and Turkey, and as Shajar al-Durr was in Egypt in the past.[7] He meant that the veiling of women does not prevent them from being heads of state or going out to work. The veil, he said, was just to protect Muslim women from Western values, which permit sexual freedom for females and homosexuality for men, both of which lead to AIDS. For him Islam is the "good" religion or the "absolute truth"; it represents virtue for women and men, which prevents adultery and disease.

Islamic positional superiority is established by avoiding criticism of the self relative to the other. The other here is the "unbeliever," *Al-Kaffar* (the devil). This attitude is viewed positively by postmodernists as reflecting cultural difference, and they separate freedom of belief from critical thinking about freedom or cultural difference. They worship freedom and difference even if they lead to cultural and economic exploitation.

The same can apply to Christian and Jewish scholars—and to so-called liberation theology movements, in which Christian scholars say that Christianity is based on love and compassion but Islam is based on justice, and justice is an abstract word that leads to violence or war. They forget that love and compassion are abstract words too and may serve in even bigger wars. Intercultural dialogue or interreligious dialogue takes place on the conference platforms at a distance from real life and its struggles. Cultural or religious comparisons are used as a proof of superiority and thus as a new instrument of domination.

Postmodern liberation theologists are widely honored in the global and local media. They are products of neocolonialism but serve as the intellectual face of the fanatical religio-political movements called religious fundamentalists. Fundamentalist religious movements do not oppose or expose neocolonial economic exploitation. They are religious movements fighting against Western values, protecting women or the Nation of Islam against Western materialism. They put more energy into veiling women and fighting against abortion than into fighting against the sale of bad meat or the shipment of nuclear waste into our country. They encourage Western banks by putting their Muslim money into them. The U.S. government calls them moderate (nonterrorist) Islamic fundamentalists and has started negotiating with them so that they can replace insufficiently flexible governments that no longer deliver what the global powers need.

Western Christian or Jewish scholars on the other hand consider Christianity or Judaism the "good" religions because they did not block the way to modernism or postmodernism, or prevent the liberation of Western women. To them Muslim women are victims of the veil, virginity, sexual inhibition, polygamy, or Islamic fundamentalist terrorism. They forget that Christian fundamentalists in the United States terrorize doctors in abortion clinics and even kill them as part of the so-called pro-life movement. This is not theological liberation but theological competition, in which each group tries to defame the other.

In 1993, in one of these conferences a young Muslim scholar from the Sudan was wearing a veil. She said that she was proud to be a Muslim veiled woman, proud that she was not Westernized or elitist; the veil was part of her authentic identity and culture, and she was a part of a women's revolution struggling against Western cultural imperialism. (I noticed that her veil was made of silk and probably imported from Harrod's in London.) For her, identity and culture had once again become an issue separate from the economic and the political. She ignored or was ignorant of the fact that women are oppressed in the three monotheistic religions (as in other religions), that class, gender, and racial discrimination are universal phenomena that originated in the slave system and have been kept alive by colonial and neocolonial powers.

Postmodernists and religious fundamentalists present themselves as new groups rejecting cultural imperialism. Today culture and religion have become the issues around which our struggles seem to center. For postmodernists "culture" is the new god. This new god takes on the aspect and form of a new dissidence, to be set against the old gods of the socialists, which were "the economy," "anticapitalism," and "antiimperialism." But if god becomes a dissident himself, we have to declare the innocence of the devil. The word *god* has to be demystified like any other word. Since the advent of "the word" in holy books, it has been used to invade other people's land (justified because this was a "promised" land), economy, and culture.

Since the beginning of human history men and women everywhere have struggled against foreign invaders and economic and cultural oppressors. They make no distinction between their minds and bodies. And they seek after song and dance just as they seek after bread and vegetables. Dissidence is a natural phenomenon in human life. We are all born dissident and creative. But we lose our creativity and dissidence partially or wholly through education and the fear that we shall be punished here or in the hereafter. We live in fear and we die in fear. Dissident people liberate themselves from fear, and they pay a price for this process of liberation. The price may be high or low but there is always a price to be paid.

Nondissident people pay a price too: the process of subordination. So if we have to pay a price anyway, why not pay the price and be liberated?

XI: Pseudodissidence

The word *dissidence* itself needs to be demystified: like the word philosophy, like the words East and West, North and South, Occident and Orient.

I met an orientalist philosopher who lives in San Francisco and writes his books in English. He is a scholar in a Californian university and is considered a dissident writer in the so-called Orient—that is, a scholar for people who do not live in the West or Occident. (I have tried to find an occidentalist philosopher or scholar, but it seems that occidentalism does not yet exist.)

In the postmodern era we meet a lot of orientalists, both white and colored. Most of them are postmodern. Some of them live in the United States and others live in Europe. None live in Egypt or Morocco or Palestine or Algeria or in other third world countries. They may go to Egypt or other countries for a short touristic visit or to make a film about Egypt or to write a book on ancient or contemporary Egypt. Then they go back home to Europe or the United States and write the book in English so that it can be read or consumed in the West. Some of these orientalists were born in Egypt or Morocco or Palestine or Algeria, but they have lived most of their life in the United States or Europe. They have not participated in any real struggle in their country of birth, or even in their country of residence.

The orientalist whom I met was invited to give a lecture in the summer of 1991 in Egypt. He was deeply imbued with orientalist arrogance and exclusivism. He wanted to be our philosopher and replace us, we who live and struggle in Egypt. He wanted to remain both in the Orient and the Occident. He insisted on the privilege of "hybridity" as his birthright. He quoted occidental postmodernists from Foucault to Derrida. He criticized U.S. cultural imperialism severely. He was smoking U.S. cigarettes. Some members of our association (which was banned a few days before his lecture) tried to meet him but he was too busy. He met the minister of culture and other ministers. He was a star on Egyptian TV as a dissident orientalist or antiorientalist.

The neocolonialist star system works very successfully, rather like the transnational corporations. The difference between the current postmodern orientalists and the old colonial orientalists is often only their country of birth or skin color. The similarities between white and colored postmodernists in the West are great. Both quote Foucault and Derrida. Both use ultra-elite complex discourse, and maintain traditional exclusionism: Orient or Occident. Both compete in the market of publishing, scholarship, the media, and CNN. Both have become a commodity; both are addicted to the production and consumption of dissident words kept at a safe distance from real struggle.

Most of them are also addicted to the production and consumption of culture and cultural products. The products that they consume are mostly American, especially Hollywood films and other U.S. mass culture. Even when they leave their homes for a trip to the third world they see only American films or TV programs. Local films and cultural productions have been overwhelmed by American products and will cease to exist as a result of the new GATT agreements. These pundits often smoke American cigarettes, in spite of the increasing antismoking campaign in the West. In Egypt smoking advertisements are increasing. The U.S. government gives grants to tobacco firms to promote smoking overseas. The sale of American cigarettes in Egypt has become as pernicious as the sale of bad meat from Europe, as pernicious as "sex-crime" films from Hollywood.

If you visit Cairo or any other city in the third world today your eye cannot miss the advertisements everywhere, the huge posters with half-naked women carrying a cigarette or a bottle of Coca-Cola in one hand and a gun in the other as they dance under the dazzling neon lights.

XII: Conclusion

It is not so difficult for us to see through and unveil the techniques and discourses of oppression and exploitation both locally and globally. After that, it is important for us to identify the new victims and the new victimizers in the neocolonial era, for we do not live in a postcolonial era as the postmodernists claim. We must struggle together both locally and globally. The local struggle must be combined with global or international struggle and solidarity. We must fight on all fronts. We must not separate the political from the sexual, economic, religious, or cultural. We must carry on a continuous resistance, a continuous dissidence, which will forge the way to a better future for *all* the peoples of the world.

NOTES

Introduction

1. "Let us go down / in the language of angels / to the broken bricks of Babel": the last stanza of Peter Huchel's poem "Begegnung" ("Meeting"), in *The Garden of Theophrastus and Other Poems,* trans. Michael Hamburger (Manchester: Carcanet, 1983), 136–37.

2. "But it does move": Galileo is supposed to have said this after he was forced by the Holy Office in 1633 to recant his "blasphemous" theory that the earth moved around the sun.

3. Callimachus, "Hymn to Zeus," l. 78, in *Callimachus, Lycophron, Aratus,* eds. A. W. Mair and G. R. Mair (London: William Heinemann, 1921).

4. Our 1995 contributors were asked to write on "the inherent dissidence of the creative word," with a further "underlying" theme of "languages of imperialism and oppression which our authors have forged into instruments of liberation."

5. For a general survey of historical change and human rights, see *Historical Change and Human Rights: The Oxford Amnesty Lectures 1994,* ed. Olwen Hufton (New York: Basic Books, 1995).

6. Laurence Sterne, *A Sentimental Journey through France and Italy,* ed. G. Petrie (Harmondsworth: Penguin, 1977), 105.

7. François Dominique Toussaint L'Ouverture (1743–1803), black freed slave and statesman, led a revolt of "mulattoes and negroes" against the French administration; "by 1801, after some years of turmoil, his highly intelligent administration had brought order and prosperity to the whole island, now unified" (*Concise Oxford Dictionary of French Literature,* ed. Joyce M. H. Reid [Oxford: Oxford University Press, 1989], s.v. "Toussaint Louverture"). Napoleon sent a military expedition under Leclerc to subdue the island and restore slavery. Toussaint L'Ouverture was captured by a trick, and died of tuberculosis in prison; resistance to Leclerc continued, and in 1803 the surviving French forces evacuated the island. For a full account, see C. L. R. James, *Toussaint L'Ouverture and the San Domingo Revolution* (New York: Vintage, 1963).

8. Jean Jacques Rousseau, *Du Contrat Social* (1762), trans. M. Cranston (Harmondsworth: Penguin, 1968), 49, opening lines of first chapter of First Book (emphasis added).

9. Gauri Viswanathan, *The Masks of Conquest* (London: Faber, 1990), 27.

10. Alexander Duff, *India and India Missions* (Edinburgh: John Johnstone, 1839), 587, in Viswanathan, 106.

11. Great Britain, *Parliamentary Papers 1852–53*, Evidence of Rev. W. Keane, 32.301, in Viswanathan, 75.

12. André Brink, *Mapmakers: Writing in a State of Siege* (London: Faber, 1983), 18–19.

13. Great Britain, *Parliamentary Papers 1852–53*, Evidence of Horace Wilson, 29.7, in Viswanathan, 40.

14. Thomas Macaulay, in Great Britain, *Parliamentary Papers 1852–1853*, Appendix K, 32.484, in Viswanathan, 41.

15. Ngũgĩ wa Thiong'o, *Decolonising the Mind. The Politics of Language in African Literature* (London: James Currey, 1994), 11.

16. Ibid.

17. Viswanathan, 113.

18. Ngũgĩ, 12.

19. Ibid., 17.

20. Viswanathan, 169.

21. This was the expression used by Masud Shadjareh, Chairman of the Human Rights Committee of the English "Muslim Parliament" on BBC's *Ghetto-Blasting* radio program (BBC Radio Scotland, February 12, 1995) in discussion with myself. He felt that double standards prevailed, citing the case of Swiss cantons in which women have no vote. The liberal inquisition, Oxford Amnesty Lectures included, was, he felt, "demonizing" Islam. I should perhaps go on record as stating that I am in favor of women having the vote and that, if Mr. Shadjareh's information is correct, the position of the Swiss cantons seems to me unacceptable. In inviting Taslima Nasreen to express opinions that she had been prevented by Islamists from expressing in her own country, OAL was not "demonizing" Islam.

22. Samuel Richardson, *Pamela*, ed. M. Kinkead-Weekes (London: Dent, 1979), 3.

23. Václav Havel, "The Power of the Powerless," in Jan Vladislav, ed., *Václav Havel or Living in Truth* (London: Faber, 1986), 95.

24. Richardson, 59.

25. Ibid., 229.

26. Ibid., 12.

27. Thomas Paine, *The Rights of Man* (1791), ed. H. Collins (Harmondsworth: Penguin, 1977), 199.

28. Pamela states that if she should lose her virtue, then "poor Pamela must be turned off and looked upon as a vile and abandoned creature; and every body would despise her, and *justly*, too, Mrs. Jervis; for she that can't keep her virtue, ought to live in disgrace." Richardson, 29.

29. Barbara Harlowe, *Resistance Literature* (London: Methuen, 1987), 139.

30. Nawal El Saadawi, *Woman at Point Zero*, trans. S. Herata (London: Zed Books, 1983), 102.

31. "He suffered as his shame swamped him." Taslima Nasreen, *Lajja*, trans. T. Gupta (Delhi: Penguin India, 1994), 203.

32. Taslima Nasreen, *Femmes, Manifestez-Vous!*, trans. S. Bhattacharja and T. Réveillé (Paris: Des Femmes, 1994), 43–48 (author's translation from the French).

33. Ibid., 53–55. However, the parallel with *Pamela* is marred if we note that the suras refer not to servants but to *slaves*.

34. "[H]e is a justice; from such a justice deliver me!" Richardson, 47.

35. Taslima Nasreen in interview with Linda Grant, "Feminist under a Fatwah," *The Guardian*, December 14, 1994.

36. Patrick Collinson conducts a survey of religion and human rights in his "Religion and Human Rights: The Case of and for Protestantism," in *Oxford Amnesty Lectures 1994*.

37. The arguments that follow are not intended to suggest that governments may never claim superior wisdom. On the contrary, as representative institutions, governments may and should undertake actions for the good of all that it would not be in the interest of any individual to undertake. These actions will then be subject to retrospective electoral censure or approval.

38. Professor Abdol Karim Soroush, Dean of the Research Institute for Human Sciences in Tehran, described as "the Martin Luther of Islam," argues points related to these, according to Robin Wright ["An Iranian Luther Shakes the Foundation of Islam," *The Guardian*, February 1, 1995]. Unfortunately, I am not acquainted with Professor Soroush's works.

39. Plato, *Republic*, III, 414C. The translation of *pseudos* is (Liddel and Scott's *Greek Lexicon*) "a lie, falsehood, untruth: a fraud, deceit," but has also been represented as "fiction"; *gennaion pseudos* is "noble lie."

40. Havel, 40.

41. Ibid., 56.

42. Ibid., 39.

43. Jan Jósef Lipski, *KOR: Workers' Defence Committee in Poland, 1976–1981*, trans. O. Amsterdamska and G. M. Moore (Berkeley: University of California Press, 1985), 215.

44. Neil Ascherson, "A Nation Mugged and Left for Dead Is Now Trying to Blow Its Brains Out," *The Independent*, March 10, 1995. To this article I owe the parallels made in this and the next paragraph.

45. Ibid.

46. A concise answer to this question can be found in Amnesty's Report on Algeria MDE 28/01/95.

47. Chinua Achebe, *Things Fall Apart* (Oxford: Heinemann, 1986), 148.

48. Frantz Fanon, *The Wretched of the Earth*, trans. C. Farrington, (Harmondsworth: Penguin, 1983), 244.

49. Edward Said, "Nationalism, Human Rights, and Interpretation," in *Freedom and Interpretation: The Oxford Amnesty Lectures 1992*, ed. Barbara Johnson (New York: Basic Books, 1993).

50. Joseph Conrad, *Heart of Darkness* (Harmondsworth: Penguin, 1976 [1902]), 10.

51. Ngũgĩ, 18. He is quoting from Eric Williams, *A History of the People of Trinidad and Tobago* (London: Deutsch, 1965), 31–32.

52. Ngũgĩ's summary (ibid., 18) directs me to this quotation from G. W. H. Hegel, *The Philosophy of History*, trans. J. Sibree (New York: Dover, 1956), 96.

53. Hegel, 93.

54. William Shakespeare, *The Tempest*, I, ii, 357–59.

55. Jean-François Lyotard, *The Post-Modern Condition: A Report on Knowledge*, trans. G. Bennington and B. Massumi (Manchester: Manchester University Press, 1986), xxiv.

56. Ludwig Wittgenstein, *On Certainty*, S109, in Roger Trigg, *Reason and Commitment* (Cambridge: Cambridge University Press, 1977), 96.

57. Trigg, 123.

58. This is a variant of the famous last sentence of Wittgenstein's *Tractatus*, in the translation of D. F. Pears and B. F. McGuinness (London: Routledge and Kegan Paul, 1961).

59. Wole Soyinka, *The Man Died: Prison Notes* (London: Vintage, 1994), xxiii.

60. William Blake, *The Marriage of Heaven and Hell*, plates 5–6.

61. Soyinka, xxiii.

62. Brink, 165.

63. André Brink: "The Failure of Censorship," first published in

Index on Censorship, 1980, reprinted in George Theiner, ed., *They Shoot Writers, Don't They?* (London: Faber, 1984), 145.

64. Percy Bysshe Shelley, "A Defence of Poetry," in *Shelley's Prose*, ed. D. L. Clark (London: Fourth Estate, 1988), 290.

65. R. W. Johnson, "R. W. Johnson Talks to the Novelist and Afrikaner Dissident, André Brink, About His Past and His Country's Future," in *The Times* (London), August 20, 1994.

66. Ralph Waldo Emerson, "Self-Reliance," from *Essays: First Series*, in *The Selected Writings of R. W. Emerson*, ed. B. Atkinson (New York: Random House, 1968), 148–49.

67. See Carlo Ginzburg's brilliant discussion, "Killing A Chinese Mandarin: The Moral Implications of Distance," in *Oxford Amnesty Lectures 1994*, 55–74.

68. Richard Rorty, "Human Rights, Rationality, and Sentimentality," in *On Human Rights: The Oxford Amnesty Lectures 1993*, eds. S. Shute and S. Hurley (New York: Basic Books, 1993).

69. Jonathan Dollimore, *Sexual Dissidence* (Oxford, Eng.: Oxford University Press, 1991), 14.

70. Ibid.

71. Rorty, 133.

72. Miklós Haraszti, *The Velvet Prison: Artists under State Socialism*, trans. K. Landesmann and S. Landesmann (London: Penguin, 1987), 74, 78, 79.

73. William Hazlitt, "Coriolanus," in *Characters of Shakespeare's Plays* (Oxford: Oxford University Press, 1939 [1817]), 56.

74. Vargas Llosa, "The Writer in Latin America," in Theiner, 163.

75. Roman Jakobson, *Questions de Poétique* (Paris: Seuil, 1973), 124 (author's translation). The translation by M. Heim in Roman Jakobson, *Selected Writings III: Poetry of Grammar, Grammar of Poetry* (The Hague/Paris/New York: Mouton, 1981), contains six fewer paragraphs than the French text; both give the same Czech original ("Co je poezie?" *Volné smery* 30 [1933–34]: 229–39).

76. Shelley, 278.

77. Jakobson, 125.

78. Shelley, 297.

79. Gabriel García Márquez quoted by Claude Couffon, "Un grand *disparu*: Haroldo Conti," *Le Monde* (Paris), January 15, 1982 (author's translation).

Notes

The Writer as Witch

1. Lucy Mair, *Witchcraft* (London: World University Library, 1973), 219.

2. Ibid.

3. Terry Eagleton, *William Shakespeare* (Oxford: Blackwell, 1986), 3.

4. Jonathan Goldberg, "Speculations: *Macbeth* and Source," in *Shakespeare Reproduced: The Text in History and Ideology*, eds. E. Howard and M. O'Connor (New York: Methuen, 1977), 247.

5. Peter Stallybrass, "*Macbeth* and Witchcraft," in *Focus on Macbeth*, ed. John Russell Brown (London: Routledge & Kegan Paul, 1982), 190.

6. Janet Farrar and Stewart Farrar, *The Witches' Goddess* (London: Robert Hale, 1987), 13.

7. Janet Adelman, "Escaping the Matrix: The Construction of Masculinity in *Macbeth* and *Coriolanus*," in *Suffocating Mothers* (New York: Routledge, 1992), 133.

8. The Nurse may be another, but her subservient social position places her on a different level. And Lady Macbeth herself, in the sleep-walking scene, also, finally, dares to acknowledge the truth.

9. The "show of eight kings" with which they conclude their provocative entertainment comprises the eight Stuart kings of Scotland (with the prudent exception of Mary Queen of Scots, beheaded by Elizabeth), while the "two-fold balls and treble sceptres" carried by some of them predict the unification of Scotland and England under James.

10. *Blick ins Chaos*, "Prospect of/gaze into chaos," the title of a volume of essays by Hermann Hesse (Zurich: Verlag Seldwyla, 1921), perhaps most famous for having been quoted by T. S. Eliot in the notes to *The Waste Land* (note to III, ll.366–76); see T. S. Eliot, *Collected Poems 1909–1962* (London: Faber and Faber, 1963). Eliot would have read the essay he cites in the *Dial* 72 (1922): 607–18, in the translation of S. Hudson. The essay ("*The Brothers Karamazov*, or the Decline of Europe") can be found in Herman Hesse, *My Belief: Essays on Life and Art*, ed. T. Ziolkowski, trans. D. Lindley and R. Mannheim (London: Paladin, 1989). —*Ed.*

11. The resonance of this phrase in South Africa derives from Father Trevor Huddlestone's critique of apartheid: *Naught for Your Comfort* (London: Collins, 1956). Huddlestone quotes "I tell you naught for your comfort" from G. K. Chesterton, "The Ballad of the White

Horse," bk. I, st. 53, l.1, in G. K. Chesterton, *Collected Poems* (London: Methuen, 1933), 233.—*Ed.*

12. Xhosa, Words of a protest song. For a fuller text, see A. Brink, *An Act of Terror* (London: Minerva, 1993), 383. —*Ed.*

Unholy Words and Terminal Censorship

1. The Ogoni are an impoverished people of about five hundred thousand living in the Niger delta. This is the area from which Shell has extracted an estimated US$30 billion worth of oil. The result for the Ogoni has been intolerable levels of air, soil, and water pollution. Oil production accounts for 95 percent of Nigerian foreign exchange earnings. The Nigerian Internal Security Task Force, sent into Rivers state in the delta in April 1994, has been responsible for unprecedented interethnic clashes, attacks on at least thirty towns and villages involving murder, rape, looting, extortion, and destruction of homes and livelihoods. Maj. Paul Okuntimo, commander of the task force, is reported to have boasted of his proficiency in killing people and of payments by Shell to himself and his men to protect oil installations. He and the Rivers state military administrator, Lt. Col. Dauda Koma, justified the use of terror at a press conference on August 2, 1994. A special court, the Civil Disturbances Tribunal, has been set up, with the power to impose the death penalty for previously noncapital crimes. Conditions of detention in Rivers state are inadequate: insufficient food, overcrowded cells, no washing facilities or exercise. The government of Gen. Sani Abacha has frequently acted with contempt for the rule of law, particularly in its efforts to stifle the free press. At present it is holding the winner of the 1993 presidential elections, Moshood Abiola, on charges of treason; his "treason" consisted in declaring himself the rightful head of state. Ken Saro-Wiwa, president of the Movement for the Survival of the Ogoni People and internationally renowned author of *Sozaboy* was held without charges for some time (sometimes chained hand and foot, and reportedly denied treatment for a heart complaint) before being accused of murder. His "judicial murder" was enacted on November 10, 1995. This is a summary of parts of Amnesty International Report AFR 44/13/94: *Nigeria*, obtainable from the International Secretariat, 1 Easton St., London WC1X 8DJ, United Kingdom. Protests should be addressed to Gen. Sani Abacha, State House, Aso Rock, Abuja, Federal Capital Territory, Nigeria, with copies to the Nigerian press. —*Ed.*

2. Odia Ofeimun, *The Vanguard* (Nigeria) [n.d.a.].

3. On February 14, 1929, members of Bugsy Moran's gang were machine-gunned in a garage in Chicago by a rival gang working for Al Capone. —*Ed.*

4. On November 18, 1978, Jim Jones, leader of the mainly Californian People's Temple cult, presided over a mass suicide at the cult's Jonestown commune in Guyana. After drinking a mixture of Kool Aid and cyanide, 913 members died. Survivors claim that some cult members were shot down trying to escape the mass suicide/massacre. —*Ed.*

5. Dr. Hastings Banda, born 1902, was one of the heroes of nationalist agitation in ex-Nyasaland, and at independence in July 1964 took power as the leader of the Malawi Congress Party. From then until the elections of June 17, 1994—imposed on him by internal and external pressure and made inevitable by the referendum on his one-party state of June 15, 1993—Banda reigned over an increasingly brutal regime that served only to pander to his megalomania. —*Ed.*

6. Mengistu was one of the group of officers who dethroned Emperor Haile Selassie on September 12, 1974; he established himself as their leader by a further coup in February 1977. The regime's attempt to impose its policies *manu militari* in the face of secessionist guerrilla warfare was accompanied by widespread starvation (sometimes seen as a policy of genocide), in particular in 1984–85. Mengistu's dictatorial regime fell in May 1991 to an offensive by the Tigré rebels, the Ethiopian People's Revolutionary Democratic Front. —*Ed.*

7. I have been unable to trace the quotation. —*Ed.*

Gay Autofiction: The Sacred and the Real

1. Guy Hocquenghem, *Homosexual Desire*, trans. D. Dangoor (Durham, N.C.: Duke University Press, 1993); Dennis Altman, *Homosexual Oppression and Liberation* (New York: Outerbridge and Dienstfey, 1971); Paul Tripp, *The Homosexual Matrix* (New York: McGraw-Hill, 1975).

2. Andrew Holleran, *Dancer from the Dance* (London: Penguin, 1978); Larry Kramer, *Faggots* (London: Methuen, 1978); Edmund White, *Nocturnes for the King of Naples* (New York: St. Martin's Press, 1979).

3. This is the Publishing Triangle, and the prize is the Bill Whitehead Award.

4. Martin Duberman, *Cures: A Gay Man's Odyssey* (New York: Plume Edition, 1991); *Stonewall* (New York: Plume Edition, 1994).

5. Eve Kosofsky Sedgwick, *Epistemology of the Closet* (Berkeley: University of California Press, 1990); *Tendencies* (Durham, N.C.: Duke University Press, 1993).

6. Jeanette Winterson, *Oranges Are Not The Only Fruit* (London: Vintage, 1991); *The Passion* (London: Penguin, 1988); *Written on The Body* (London: Vintage, 1993).

7. Rita Mae Brown, *Rubyfruit Jungle* (1973) (London: Penguin, 1994); *The Hand That Cradles The Rock* (New York: New York University Press, 1971); *Six of One* (New York: Harper & Row, 1978); *Southern Discomfort* (New York: Harper & Row, 1982).

8. Paul Monette, *Borrowed Time* (London: Flamingo, 1988); *Becoming a Man* (London: Abacus, 1992).

9. David Leavitt, *The Lost Language of Cranes* (London: Viking, 1986); *Equal Affections* (London: Penguin, 1989).

10. Armistead Maupin, *Tales of the City, More Tales of the City, Further Tales of the City: An Omnibus* (London: Chatto & Windus, 1989).

11. Alan Hollinghurst, *The Swimming Pool Library* (London: Penguin, London, 1988); *The Folding Star* (London: Chatto & Windus, 1994).

12. Paul Bailey, *An Immaculate Mistake* (Harmondsworth: Penguin, 1991).

13. Adam Mars-Jones, *Monopolies of Loss* (London: Faber, 1992); *The Waters of Thirst* (London: Faber, 1993).

14. Hubert Fichte, *Versuch über die Pubertät* (Frankfurt: Fischer Taschenbuch Verlag, 1976); *The Orphanage*, trans. M. Chalmers (London: Serpent's Tail, 1990); *Detlev's Imitations*, trans. M. Chalmers (London: Serpent's Tail, 1992).

15. Dominique Fernandez, *Le Rapt de Ganymède* (Paris: Grasset, 1989); Tony Duvert, *When Jonathan Died*, trans. D. R. Roberts (London: Gay Mens Press, 1991); Renaud Camus, *Tricks*, trans. R. Howard (New York: St. Martin's Press, 1991).

16. Hervé Guibert, *To The Friend Who Did Not Save My Life*, trans. L. Coverdale (London: Quartet, 1991); Guy Hocquenghem, *L'Amour en relief* (Paris: Albin Michel, 1982); Gilles Barbedette, *Baltimore* (Paris: Gallimard, 1991).

17. Angelo Rinaldi, *Les Jardins du consulat* (Paris: Gallimard, 1991); Hector Bianciotti, *Sans la Miséricorde de Christ* (Paris: Gallimard, 1987).

18. Geneviève Pastre, *De l'amour lesbien* (Paris: Horay, 1980).

19. From the Italian, *fare bella figura*: show to advantage, cut a fine figure. —*Ed.*

20. Pier Vittorio Tondelli, *Pao Pao* (Milan: Feltrinelli, 1989); *Separate Rooms*, trans. S. Pleasance (London: Serpent's Tail, 1992); Aldo Busi, *The Standard Life of a Temporary Pantyhose Salesman*, trans. R. Rosenthal (London: Faber, 1988); *Sodomies in Sevenpoint*, trans. S. Hood (London: Faber, 1993).

21. Patrick Chamoiseau, *Texaco* (Paris: Gallimard, 1992).

22. Jean Genet, *Querelle of Brest*, trans. G. Stretham (London: Paladin, 1987).

23. Letter to Jean-Paul Sartre, quoted in *Le Dictionnaire Gay*, ed. Lionel Povert (Paris: J. Granchet, 1994), 234.

24. Jean Genet, *A Prisoner of Love*, trans. B. Bray (London: Picador, 1992).

25. André Gide, *Corydon*, trans. R. Howard (New York: Farrar, Straus & Giroux, 1983), Dialogue II–III; see also Patrick Pollard, *André Gide: Homosexual Moralist* (New Haven: Yale University Press, 1991), 117.

26. Marcel Proust, *Remembrance of Things Past*, vol. 4, *Sodom and Gomorrah*, trans. C. K. Scott-Moncrieff (London: Chatto & Windus, 1992), 2–3ff.

27. Théophile Gautier, "Notice" (February 20, 1868) to *Les Fleurs du Mal*, in Charles Baudelaire, *Oeuvres complètes*, vol. 1 (Paris: Calmann-Lévy, n.d.), 26 (Edmund White's translation).

28. Ibid. Quoted without attribution by Théophile Gautier.

29. Michel Foucault, "What Is an Author?" trans. J. V. Harari, in *The Foucault Reader*, ed. Paul Rabinow (New York: Pantheon Books, 1984), 91.

30. Harold Rosenberg, *Tradition of the New* (New York: Da Capo Press, 1994).

31. Honoré de Balzac, *A Harlot High and Low*, trans. R. Heppenstall (Harmondsworth: Penguin, 1970), 286.

32. See Mikhail Mikhailovich Bakhtin, "The Dialogic Idea as Novelistic Image," in *The Bakhtin Reader*, ed. Pam Morris (London: Edward Arnold, 1994), 97.

33. John Rechy, *City of Night* (New York: Grove/Atlantic, 1988).

34. Samuel Delany, *The Mad Man* (New York: Richard Kasak, 1994).

35. Pai Hsien-Yung, *Crystal Boys*, trans. Howard Goldblatt (New York: Gay Sunshine, 1990).

36. René de Ceccaty, *Violette Leduc: éloge de la bâtarde* (Paris: Stock, 1994).

37. See Nathalie Heinich, "Martyrologie de l'art moderne: Van Gogh et l'irruption de la faute," in *L'Art moderne et la question du sacré*, ed. Jean-Jacques Nillès (Paris: Les Editions du Cerf, 1993).

38. Margery Kempe (c. 1373–c. 1440), daughter of a mayor of King's Lynn, was married in 1393, and went on a series of pilgrimages after having borne fourteen children. She is thought to have dictated the *Book of Margery Kempe* in 1432–c. 1436. Its first publication in modern English was in 1936; the Early English Text Society published the Middle English original (ed. Professor Sandford Brown Meed) in 1940. —*Ed.*

39. Robert Glück, *Margery Kempe* (London: Serpent's Tail, 1994).

40. Arthur Schopenhauer, *The World as Will and Representation*, vol. 1, trans. E. F. J. Payne (New York: Dover, 1969), 247.

41. Paul Veyne, *Did the Greeks Believe in Their Myths? An Essay on the Constitutive Imagination*, trans. P. Wissing (Chicago: University of Chicago Press, 1988), 121.

The Oppressor and the Oppressed

1. Bankim Chandra, *Banglar Itihas Samparke Koetki Katha*, in Bankim Chandra, *Collected Works*, ed. Jogesh Chandra (Calcutta: Sahittay Sangsad, 1955), 377.

2. K. M. Panikkar, *Asia and Western Dominance: The Vasco da Gama Era of Asian History* (London: George Allen & Unwin, 1953), 101.

3. Macaulay's *Minute* of February 2, 1835, to the Governor-General's Council, quoted in *History and Culture of the Indian People*, vol. 10, *British Paramountcy and the Indian Renaissance*, ed. R. C. Majumdar (Bombay: Bharatiya Vidya Bhavan, 1965), 83.

4. Rammohun Roy (attributed), "Address to Lord William Bentinck," in *Collected Works in English*, vol. 2, ed. J. C. Ghose (Delhi: Cosmo Publications, 1992), 474.

5. Rammohun Roy, "Petition Against the Press Regulation to the King in Council," in ibid., 457.

6. Macaulay, Speech to the House of Commons, in *History and Culture of the Indian People*, vol. 10, 37.

7. Sir Percival Griffiths, *The British Impact on India* (London, 1952), 245, quoted in ibid., 37.

8. *History and Culture of the Indian People*, vol. 10, 37. (The quotation continues: "The young men brought up in our seminaries . . . have

no notion of any improvement but such as rivets their connection with the English and makes them dependent on English protection and instruction," making even clearer the spirit in which education was offered. —*Ed.*)

9. Pearychand Mitra, *Life of David Hare* (Calcutta, 1949), quoted in ibid., 39.

10. B. B. Majumdar, *History of Political Thought. From Rammohun to Dayananda*, vol. 1, *Bengal* (Calcutta, 1934), 83.

11. See ibid., 83.

12. A Hindu correspondent of *The Englishman*, May 1836, in ibid., 79–80.

13. Ibid., 86. (This refers to the Academic Association whose foundation [1828] was inspired by Derozio. —*Ed.*)

14. This was the Society for the Acquisition of General Knowledge, founded 1836; the event took place on February 8, 1843. See *History and Culture of the Indian People*, vol. 10, 40–41. —*Ed.*

15. Ibid., 41.

16. The *tricouleur* was hoisted with the Union Jack after a grand banquet given by the commanders of French vessels visiting Bengal. See B. B. Majumdar, *History of Political Thought*, 83–84. —*Ed.*

17. Geoffrey Moorehouse, *India Britannica* (London: Harvill Press, 1983), 145.

18. Aurobindo Ghose was born in 1872 in Calcutta, and educated in India and at Cambridge. He was politically active in 1902–1910. Imprisoned for nationalist agitation in 1908, he took residence in the then French colony of Pondichéry where he wrote the religious works for which he is best known, including *The Life Divine* (1940), *The Human Cycle* (1949). He died in 1950. —*Ed.*

19. See introduction (paragraph 3 and following) for an account of Bose's life. —*Ed.*

20. Sukumar Sen, "Women's Dialect in Bengali," *Journal of the Department of Letters* (University of Calcutta) 18 (1929):1.

21. This is Otto Jespersen's conclusion (*Language, Its Nature, Development and Origin* [London: Allen and Unwin, 1968], 241), which Sen cites and disputes in the 1929 edition. Taslima Nasreen refers to Sen, *Women's Dialect in Bengali* (Calcutta: Jynasa, 1979), which I have not been able to consult. Sen suggests that "Prakrit speech being considered more sweet and mellow than Sanskrit, female characters in the dramas (heroines and high class women) speak that language." Jespersen's view seems tenable, especially as Sen prefaces his remarks above with

the observation that "Woman is concerned with her home and children and is essentially timid and superstitious." —*Ed.*

22. Sen, 57–58. (The last proverb was added for the 1979 edition of *Women's Dialect in Bengali.* —*Ed.*)

23. Malavika Karlekar, *Voices from Within: Early Personal Narratives by Bengali Women* (Delhi: Oxford University Press, 1991), 11.

24. Ibid., 127.

25. Ibid., 135.

26. Begum Rokeya, *Sampadaker Nibedon*, in Begum Rokeya, *Collected Works*, ed. Abdul Kadir (Dhaka: Bangla Academy, 1984), 11.

27. Karlekar, 25n2.

28. Taslima Nasreen, *Amar Kichu Jai Ase Na*, trans. Carolyne Wright (Dhaka: Vidayprakash, 1990), 9.

On Chaos

1. Harold Bloom, *The Western Canon: The Books and The Schools of The Ages* (London: Macmillan, 1994).

2. John Jay Chapman, "Trends in Popular Thought," in *New Horizons in American Life* (New York: Columbia University Press, 1932), 44; reprinted in *Arion* (Spring/Fall 1992/93), 47. (The essay was not reprinted integrally in *Arion*, where it does begin thus. In *New Horizons* it begins: "This is an age when any man must feel embarrassed to preach on what is on everyone's mind—war, peace, religion, art, industry, social life—for they all point to the same text on the blackboard, to the impending unification of the human race upon the globe: 'Ye are members of one another.' " —*Ed.*)

3. Ibid., 44–45 (*Arion*, 47).

4. Ibid., 45 (*Arion*, 48). (The Emerson quotation seems likely to be a misremembered version of "Always do what you are afraid to do," from "Heroism," in *Essays: First Series*, in *The Selected Writings of Ralph Waldo Emerson*, ed. B. Atkinson [New York: Random House, 1968], 258.) —*Ed.*

5. Previously unpublished essay by J. J. Chapman, "Plato," in the possession of the Houghton Library of Harvard University (bMS Am 1854 [6522]), in *Arion*, 66, by permission of the Houghton Library, Harvard University. Plato compares philosophy to a raft in *Phaedo*, 85c-d.

6. Ibid., 67–68.

7. Ibid., 93–95.

8. Ibid., 96.

9. Both quotations are from *Flaubert-Sand: The Correspondence,* trans. F. Steegmuller and B. Bray. Based on the French edition by Alphonse Jacobs (London: Harvill, 1993): letter 259, August 3, 1870, 208.

10. Ibid., letter 275, April 28, 1871, 226.

11. Ibid., letter 276, April 30, 1871, 228.

12. Ibid., letter 289, October 25, 1871, 249.

13. Ibid., letter 275, April 28, 1871, 227.

14. Jean Monnet (1899–1979), French economist and civil servant, regarded as "the father of the European Community." Monnet prepared the Schuman Plan, which formed the basis of the pioneering European Coal and Steel Community, of which he was the first president, 1952–1955. The ECSC led to the creation of the European Economic Community in 1957 and the European Community in 1967. Jacques Delors (b. 1925), French economist and politician, Minister of Economics, 1981–1984, and influential president of the European Commission, 1985–1995. —*Ed.*

15. The reference is to Abraham Lincoln's Gettysburg Address: "[W]e here highly resolve . . . that the nation shall have a new birth of freedom." For Mr. Vidal, this was the *birth* of the Union and not a rebirth. —*Ed.*

Dissidence and Creativity

1. Egypt was declared a "protectorate" in 1914, when Britain went to war with Turkey; it had been under English "administration" since the 1882 invasion, the pretext for which had been anti-European demonstrations. —*Ed.*

2. The title "khedive" was that of viceroy under Ottoman suzerainty. —*Ed.*

3. I am unable to trace any joint publication by Foucault and Deleuze, or to trace this quotation under either name. —*Ed.*

4. *Al-'arabi,* Cairo, November 14, 1994, 13.

5. *Ruz al-yusif,* November 21, 1994, 18.

6. Hypatia was "torn to pieces" in A.D. 415 "by a mob of Christians at the instigation of their bishop (later Saint) Cyril" (*The Oxford Classical Dictionary,* 2d ed., s.v. "Hypatia"). She was an influential

teacher of the pagan Neoplatonist philosophy, who revised her father Theon's *Commentary on the Almagest*. In Chapter XLVII of *The Decline and Fall of the Roman Empire* (New York: Everyman's, 1993), Gibbon specifies Cyril's motive as jealousy of her influence: "On a fatal day, in the holy season of Lent, Hypatia was torn from her chariot, stripped naked, dragged to the church, and inhumanly butchered by the hands of Peter the reader and a troop of savage and merciless fanatics; her flesh was scraped from her bones with sharp oyster-shells, and her quivering limbs were delivered to the flames" (vol. 5, 14–15). The date of destruction of the great library of Alexandria is a matter of controversy. Plutarch (*Caes.* 49) states that it occurred when Caesar was besieged in Alexandria in A.D. 48. Dio Cassius (42.38) contradicts this. Other accounts suggest that it was destroyed during the civil war that occurred under Aurelian in the late third century A.D., and its "daughter library," which had been founded by Ptolemy III in 235 B.C., was destroyed by the Christians in A.D. 391. —*Ed.*

7. Shajar al-Durr was sent by the caliph of Baghdad as a gift to Al-Malik al-Salih, the sultan of Egypt, who was the first of the Egyptian Ayyubids to recruit Turkish Mamluks on a large scale as mercenaries. Shajar al-Durr bore him a son, Turan-Shah, and gained considerable influence in the affairs of the kingdom. In 1249 Al-Malik al-Salih was killed in battle with the Crusaders. Turan-Shah sought to replace Al-Malik al-Salih's Mamluks with his own, and to weaken Shajar al-Durr's position. In 1250 a group of Mamluks killed Turan-Shah and proclaimed Shajar al-Durr sultan. Faced with the opposition of the other Ayyubid princes, she appointed a commander-in-chief, the Amir Aybeg, who married her and became sultan. He contrived to alienate both Mamluks and wife, and she arranged his murder on April 12, 1257. She herself was murdered three days later. (Condensed from the *Cambridge History of Islam*, eds. P. M. Holt, A. K. S. Lanston, and B. Lewis [Cambridge, Eng.: Cambridge University Press, 1977], s.v. "Shajar al-Durr"). —*Ed.*

CONTRIBUTORS

ANDRÉ BRINK, South African novelist and essayist, *Chevalier* of the *Légion d'honneur* and *Commandeur de l'Ordre des Arts et des Lettres*, is Professor of English at the University of Cape Town. His novels include *An Instant in the Wind*, *A Dry White Season*, *Looking on Darkness*, *An Act of Terror*, and *On the Contrary*.

WOLE SOYINKA, Nigerian poet, playwright, novelist, critic, and one of the leaders of the Nigerian opposition, currently lives in exile. He won the Nobel Prize for Literature in 1986. His plays include *Madmen and Specialists* and *Death and the King's Horseman*; his novels include *The Interpreters* and *Season of Anomy*; his poetry includes *Idanre and Other Poems* and *Mandela's Earth*; and his memoirs include *Aké* and *Ìsarà*.

EDMUND WHITE, gay American novelist, essayist, and biographer, lives in Paris. His novels include *Nocturnes for the King of Naples*, *A Boy's Own Story*, *Caracole*, *Forgetting Elena*, and *The Beautiful Room Is Empty*. He is the biographer of Genet.

TASLIMA NASREEN, feminist Bangladeshi doctor, poet, novelist, essayist, and columnist, currently lives in exile under a *fatwa*. Her novels include *Lajja* (Shame) and *Fera* (Return). Her nonfiction publications include *Nirbachito Column* (Selected Columns) and six volumes of poetry. She won the Ananda Award in 1992 and the Sakharov Prize in 1994.

GORE VIDAL, American political activist, playwright, novelist, and essayist, was co-chairman of the People's Party 1970–1972. His novels include *The City and the Pillar*, *Julian*, *Washington DC*, *Myra Breckenridge*, *Burr*, and *Lincoln*. His essays include *Rocking the Boat*, *Matters of Fact and Fiction*, *Screening History*, *A View from the Diner's Club*, and *Dark Green, Bright Red*.

NAWAL EL SAADAWI, feminist Egyptian doctor, political activist, novelist, and essayist, currently lives in exile in the United States. Her fiction includes *Woman at Point Zero, God Dies by the Nile, Death of an Ex-Minister,* and *She Has No Place in Paradise.* Her nonfiction includes *Women and Sex, The Hidden Face of Eve: Women in the Arab World,* and *Memoirs from the Women's Prison.*

CHRIS MILLER, English translator and critic, is one of the founders of the Oxford Amnesty Lectures.

INDEX

194

Index

Index

Index

Index